Aliens from the Future

Sara Luker

Contents

CHAPTER 1

In Sonoma County, California, many people were going on with their lives. Within the county, there was the building of Child Protective Services. The building had two sections; one was the main headquarters where social workers worked, and the other was where some of the foster children lived. A young adolescent girl was seventeen years old in one of the rooms. She stood at 5'5 tall; her skin was medium olive, and her shoulder-length hair was curly and pitch black. Her eyes were light brown, and her small lips were pale pink. The young lady also had a hin appearance that made her look sick because of the constant neglect from living in the foster care system. She was also of African and Mexican descent.

CHAPTER 2

Y esele POV

In a couple of weeks, I will turn eighteen. It should be the happiest day of anyone's life, but for me, I felt scared. Ever since I could remember, I have been in the foster care system. I never knew my parents, but according to the social worker, my mother was a drug addict prostitute, and my father was one of her many clients.

I have been in many foster families; a few were nice, but others were not. I escaped from being abused by many of the families. There were times when I hated my life and thought of suicide. I was scared to turn eighteen because I had no home and how to apply for jobs. On the other hand, I would be free from the foster care system, and I don't have to suffer anymore.

At the moment, I am in my room looking at the top bunk bed that used to belong to my former roommate, who turned eighteen and left. She was given a job at a local restaurant. In a sense, I was taught a bit about some work skills, most basic stuff. Many who were going to leave the foster care system were taught how to do low-end jobs. That is how we are viewed, worthless. We aren't given opportunities as others. I have always wanted to be a social worker to help children in my situation. I want to advocate for them and help them. No child should be in this kind of system.

My thoughts were interrupted when there was a knock on the door. Someone opened the door. It was my social worker, Karen. She's in her fifties; there were times when I viewed her as a mother figure. She is of African descent with many wrinkles on her face and parts of her hands. Karen nicely combed her gray curly hair; she wore her professional clothing. Karen always treated and respected me; not many social workers were like her. The older woman motivated me to be like her.

I saw her smile. "Yesele, I have news for you. You are to be adopted."

I felt my heart skipping a beat, and I immediately sat up. "W-What!?"

"Yes, child. There is a couple that wants to adopt you. Don't worry; we did a background search on them, and they are in the clear," she said with a smile on her face.

"I-I don't u-understand! They could have the younger kids. I will turn eighteen soon; I'd be worthless to them!"

Karen stood silently and looked the other way; she looked sad and slightly uncomfortable. Yet, her expression changed to a happier one. "They don't see it that way. Come on, get ready. The couple has signed the paperwork; they are waiting for you. I'll see you in a bit."

Before I could ask any more questions, she left. Strange, but I also felt happy at the same time. A family would give me a chance to show that I could prove myself. I began to pack the little belongings I had. So many thoughts were going through my head.

How was my new family?

Will they like me?

Will I go to college?

Will my dreams come true?

About thirty minutes, I was finished, got out of my room, and went towards the office where Karen awaited me. Inside the office, there was a man and a woman. Both looked to be in their early fifties and eyed me with seriousness. I looked back at Karen, who had a smile, but something was off about the smile.

She looked sad and scared. "Yesele, this is Mr. and Mrs. Heil. They will be your family from now on."

The woman walked toward me and smiled. She looked to be at least five feet tall and of Caucasian descent. Her light blonde hair was wrapped in a nice bun. There were slight wrinkles on her face since she had a bit of heavy makeup, which made her look older than her actual age. Her eyes were blue and were a bit chunky, appearance-wise. "Oh, you are so beautiful, Yesele. I have always wanted a daughter. I could never have children of my own, and in the end, my husband and I decided to adopt.

I raised an eyebrow. "Th-Thank you. Why did you choose me?" I couldn't help but feel a bit suspicious.

Karen flinched and immediately cleared her throat. "Yesele, that-"

Mrs. Heil raised her hand. "It's alright. We are old, Yesele. We worry that if we have a young child and die soon, there will be no one to take care of the child. We thought it was best to have a grown child." The older woman smiled. " I can see you are a good young lady, and you have high aspirations. We couldn't have children, even though we did try."

I put my arms around myself. I felt bad for asking. This couple couldn't have children of their own. How terrible, but I felt happy. I am given a chance to prove that I am a good choice.

"My husband and I will do everything to give you a great future. We even saved up money for your education if you accept."

The woman sounded so sincere; the older man smiled and nodded. Maybe it would not be so bad after all. "Okay, I would like that."

Mrs. Heil smiled and hugged me.

Karen gave me the paperwork to sign, which I signed up. Karen and I hugged one another, and I went off with the couple. As I left, I heard Karen cry. She probably was going to miss me as I would miss her.

....

The drive was enjoyable for Yesele. Mr. and Mrs. Heil asked about her likes, dislikes, aspirations, etc. The young lady felt happy that she was given a second chance. Mr. Heil kept driving on the road that led to the woods. "Yesele, you have so many goals in life, and I am sorry that you had to live such a hard life. My wife and I looked at so many prospects, but when we looked at your picture, we knew that you were a perfect addition to our family."

Yesele blushed at Mr. Heil's comment. Then, Yesele looked by the window and saw the many trees, making her feel at ease and calm. About ten minutes into the road by trees, the car moved to the left, which led to a bumpy road. Yesele was confused. "Where are we going?"

The couple did not look at her. "To your new home, my dear. We live in the woods, but don't worry; other people also live there. It is a little community of people that don't like to live in the city and prefer mother nature."

The young woman nodded and decided not to speak more. However, the more Mr. Heil drove deeper and deeper into the woods, the more she began to feel nervous and unsafe. As they went on, Yesele saw a sign that said 'Monte Rio.' In what felt like an eternity, Yesele saw something from afar. It was a huge concrete building with so many people, but they had weapons and looked like soldiers.

"What is-?"

Mrs. Heil turned to her and smiled. "Welcome to your new home, the Bohemian Grove. Yesele, your participation is vital for our cause."

Mr. Heil parked the car. Yesele noticed the soldier's eyes through the window. A soldier walked forward and opened the car door, but she did not get out. Her eyes were wide open, and she moved away from the soldiers. "Who are you!?"

The couple got out of the car. Mrs. Heil opened the side of the vehicle that Yesele was in. "You should get out now, or else you will be forced," she said sternly.

The young woman trembled. Suddenly, some soldiers held Yesele's arms and pulled her out. She yelped out and was then forced into the facility. Yesele had never felt so confused and terrified in her life. As she went inside, there were many people with different types of technology that she had never seen before and weapons that she thought could never exist.

She dared not speak, for Yesele was afraid of the consequences. As she was taken deeper into the facility, the soldiers stopped midway and forced her to see something. Her eyes became wide open in horror; her lips were also wide open.

It was a being that was out of this world. It was taller than any man she had ever seen, about 7 feet tall. The being had the body of a man but had reptile-like aqua skin with many scars; its eyes were golden reptile-like. The being had a long tail with small black horns. It also had a human male-like face, but teeth stuck out from its lips. "W-Wh-What in the world!?"

"Yes, it is a lovely creature, isn't it?" asked a masculine voice.

Yesele saw a man who looked to be in his early forties. He had faded blonde hair, blue eyes, a couple of wrinkles, and aging spots on his light skin, making him look more elderly. The man was tall as Yesele and slightly overweight. The man walked towards her in a white coat, making him look like a doctor. He smiled at her. "You must be Yesele. I bid you welcome to this facility. I am Dr. Antony, and that creature is an alien since you asked." He chuckled. "I am sure you have many questions, and I will answer them." He motioned the soldiers to take Yesele to his office, which they did.

Yesele turned to look at the creature as she was led away.

....

"This is my colleague, Dr. Logan. We are very pleased to have you in this facility, it took us a while to have a test subject, but the wait was worthwhile."

Dr. Logan was shorter than Dr. Antony; he was overweight and completely bald. His face and hands had many wrinkles and age spots; he also had large 1980s glasses. Dr. Logan was in his late forties but looked older. He wore tight clothes that made his face hang out. His teeth were yellow, and he had a foul body odor.

Yesele felt her body tremble; her heart was beating in fear. "I-I don't understand. What do you mean by test subject? That couple was not adopting me?" she asked quietly, terrified.

Dr. Logan chuckled. "They were not a couple; they only played the part. I am sure they acted beautifully since you believed them. In a sense, you are adopted by us. You are part of our family."

The young woman felt her eyes forming tears; she put her arms around herself. "I-I want to go back. I don't want to be here! I want to call Karen!"

The two scientists sighed. Dr. Antony got a water bottle and gave it to the trembling orphan. "You are not going back, young one. We have come so far to achieve you. Karen will not do anything. She had already signed the paperwork; she was paid handsomely. If you were to go back, we would take our money back." He chuckled. "Yet, we will eventually kill her. Money cannot always keep people silent."

Tears fell from Yesele's eyes. "She would never!"

"She did, that foolish old hag was filled with debt, and her desperation got the best of her. You must understand that the world is cruel; people will do anything for themselves. Karen cared more for herself than for you." Dr. Logan smiled. "But don't worry, that woman who betrayed you will be no more. She knows of us and must be gone."

Yesele couldn't hold it back. She cried. The young woman felt alone, scared, and lost.

"Don't cry, young one. We will take good care of you. If you obey our orders, you will live well. You have a huge responsibility. Did you see the alien?"

"Th-That was an alien?"

"Yes, quite an exquisite specimen we found. We learned many things about it, and we want to make clones. However, our technology is not advanced enough to make clones, so we developed another solution. With that in mind, we need your help," explained Dr. Antony.

"What am I supposed to do?"

The scientists smiled. "Why, you will bear its offspring. You will mate with it."

The young woman gasped in horror. "No! No! I will not do that! I would rather die! Please no!"

"Don't worry; we will not harm you. We will make sure of it. Unless you want to suffer like the alien, being beaten, tortured until you submit, or we could drug you so you can enjoy the act. The choice is yours, young one." Dr. Antony clapped his hands. " I am sure this will be a lot to take in; you will be taken to your room. Guards."

Two guards got a hold of Yesele and dragged her out of the office to her room. Many workers in the facility heard her screams.

Chapter 3

It was nothing but a dream.

Karen lied and sold her to the government. A tear dripped from her right eye. Then, Yesele heard a loud screech, and it made her cringe. She slowly got off her bed and went to the door. With the small window, she could see what was happening from afar.

Guards told the alien commands, but the alien refused to follow their orders. As a consequence, the alien was teased and kicked. The alien screeched with pain; Yesele watched everything that was happening. She was horrified. It made the young woman wonder how long the alien has been locked in the facility.

It made her heart break for the alien. Yesele walked back and forth. "Maybe we're not so different after all." She sat on her bed, rocking back and forth as Yesele heard the alien's screeching throughout the day.

....

The Next Day

Yesele was taken to the showers by female guards, who stood outside, waiting for her. The young woman felt the warm water trickle down her nude body. Even though she saw the alien's abuse, Yesele still felt afraid.

She wanted to escape but knew it would be impossible; the scientists would do everything to prevent her from escaping, even killing her. Yesele wanted to feel no fear of death but still wanted to live. On the other hand, the scientist would get another woman to complete their experimentation.

Then, the female guards entered the shower room, ordered Yesele to dress, and await orders in her room. Two hours passed; it felt like torture for Yesele, not knowing if she would be given to the alien or not. Ten minutes later, the door to her room opened. Dr. Antony and Logan entered, and the guards waited outside.

"It's time, young lady," said Dr. Antony.

Yesele put her arms around herself. "I don't want to go."

"Oh, my dear. You don't have a choice in the matter. If you refuse, then you'll be forced. I would rather give you some dignity."

"Dignity? You took it away from me when I first entered this hellhole."

Dr. Antony chuckled. "Hellhole, you say? You've been treated a bit more human than being in foster care. Even if we didn't bring you here, do you think you'd still have your dignity?

The world is a cruel place, my dear. You have always been in the system; you would have worked in low-income jobs. Your social status, race, and sex would have judged the outside world. You would have had no opportunities."

Yesele trembled as she felt his words pierce her heart. Then, two guards entered and forced her out of her room, leading her to a large room. The room was dark, but only a couple of small bulbs lit the room dimly. Yesele was forcibly undressed by the guards and pushed in. She lost her footing and fell to the floor.

"Don't worry. No one will watch the action. As I said, we will give you dignity since you are doing so much for us. I've been told that you're still a virgin. Don't worry; I'm certain having intercourse with an alien is similar to human intercourse. The alien won't hurt you. Be confident, and hopefully, you'll get pregnant on the first try. If not, then you'll have to try again." Dr. Antony then closed the doors, leaving the young woman alone.

Yesele stood and then sat by the wall, wrapping her arms around herself. Then, the heavy doors opened once again. The alien was motioned inside by a rover, tied up by chains. Once the heavy doors were closed shut, the chains were automatically undone. The young woman's eyes were wide with horror. She wanted to scream, but a loud squeal escaped her lips. This got the alien's attention; it looked at her. He got off the rover and slowly walked toward the human female.

"No! Don't get any closer!"

The alien stopped as he was a couple of inches away from her. He noticed Yesele trembling and realized that she was afraid of him. The alien backed away only a little. Yesele slowly glanced at the alien and saw it standing there. He didn't move a muscle, but it looked at her. She tried to make out his expression. She then heard a slight groan, and the alien knelt, bowing his head.

It confused Yesele, but the realization hit her; the alien was trying to tell her that he would not hurt her. Then, the memories of watching him being tortured came to her; his screeches of pain were hard to forget. She slowly turned to him but still covered herself with her arms. "I saw what they did to you. How long have you been trapped here?"

The alien slowly raised his head, looking at her. He could not communicate with her, but he did understand her. "I was raised in the system, never having a proper family and home. I was lied to, given false hope, and brought here. You and I aren't different in certain circumstances. They want us to mate, even though we hardly know one another, and I'm scared."

Then, the alien slowly stood and walked towards her but kept his distance. Yesele didn't back away. "Even though I don't want this, these monsters will find a way to get what they want. I guess we both can't escape." She slowly walked to the alien and stopped in front of him. Yesele lowered her hands, exposing all of her body, and touched his face; the alien had rough skin. He also touched her face and liked how soft she felt. Even though the alien couldn't speak the human language, he understood it to an extent.

He knew what the human scientists wanted them to do. The alien didn't want to; he was afraid that he would harm Yesele.

She slowly hugged him as tears dripped from her eyes. "Please try to be gentle; I've never done this before."

The alien gave out a small groan; he slowly touched her face; with his other hand, he trailed down on her back, feeling her soft skin. Yesele slightly flinched; she tried to calm down. Then, the alien held her hand, putting them on his chest. He motioned her hands all over his chest. She felt a growl on his chest.

Yesele began to calm her nerves as she realized that the alien was being gentle with her. He didn't want to hurt her. As she looked down, she saw it; the alien's cock. His cock was erect by her touch alone; it was at least 8 inches. Yesele could feel some of her juice dripping from her entrance.

She gathered her courage, got a hold of the alien's cock, and began to stroke it. The alien was shocked by her sudden action, but he let her continue. A feeling of pleasure went through his entire body; he let out a growl. He couldn't take it anymore; the alien got a hold of Yesele, put her back on the wall, and lifted her. Her vagina was in front of the alien's face. The alien began to lick her entrance.

"Oh my...!" Yesele felt his tongue inside her, making her even wetter. She trembled from the pleasure. His tongue was a little deeper. "I feel...! I feel that I'm going to cum!" After a few more licks, Yesele came on the alien's tongue.

The alien felt a bit of his pre-cum from the tip of his erect cock. He couldn't contain himself anymore. He lowered her down; the tip of his cock touched her entrance. The alien looked at Yesele as she did the same; she gave him the nod. Slowly, he motioned his cock inside of her. Yesele held onto his shoulder. The young woman felt his cock stretching her virgin walls.

Half of his cock was inside her; she felt his tip on her charm point. The alien could tell that Yesele was in pain; he didn't move as he let her get used to his length. However, it was challenging to be still. The alien felt her wet walls clenching and squeezing his cock; a growl escaped his lips. Moments later, the pain disappeared, and Yesele began to feel pleasure. She nodded to him slowly; the alien continued to move his waist upward.

The squishing of her wet entrance was heard, making the alien growl in pleasure and excitement. He thrust his cock upward, making his cock go deeper. Yesele moaned as her nails almost dug into his shoulders. With every thrust he made, Yesele's breast bounced, and her juices dripped down to his cock.

Yesele came the third time; she was getting weaker. "So good, I can't! I can't hold on much more!" Her arms were weak and let go, but the alien still held onto her; her breast was in front of his face. This excited the alien even more; his thrust became more erratic that his ball sack slapped parts of her ass and entrance.

The alien let out a loud groan as he came inside her; his body shook from the pleasure. Both breathed heavily. The alien laid Yesele on the floor; he took his cock out of her as he lay next to her.

The two looked at one another, smiling at one another. However, they knew it was a matter of time before the guards would separate them again.

CHAPTER 4

"**I** -I am what?"

"I told you that you are pregnant. Why are you surprised? You did mate with the alien; things like this happen," the female scientist said rudely.

Yesele put her hand over her womb as she was in shock. The guards then motioned her out of the office and her room. She was alone in her room as so many thoughts went through her mind. "I am pregnant."

Silence reigned in her room. It had only been three days since she and the alien mated, and she was carrying their child. To her surprise, she did not feel fear or dread but felt a sense of protection and unconditional love for her unborn child. It was strange to her, never had she felt these feelings before. Yesele always wanted to be protected and loved by another, by a family. As she sat quietly, her thoughts trailed to her mate and what would happen.

The scientists had her results; everyone in the facility would know of her pregnancy. Since that was the case, Yesele began to feel worried for the safety of her unborn child. The young lady did not want her child to suffer like her and the alien. She never knew how it was to have a family. Yesele wanted her unborn child to live a better life. Yesele decided that she had to speak with the alien.

....

A Week Later

The alien was in his prison; he gave the scientists a difficult time. The scientists were unable to control him to do experiments. The alien wanted to see his mate. For him, it felt like an eternity.

The scientist picked up on this; they permitted Yesele to see him and calm him down.

The two were given a room with guards keeping watch outside the windows.

The two were face to face and were happy to see one another. Yesele went to him. The alien was chained and unable to move. The human female hugged him, and the alien made a soft noise.

"I don't have much time, but I wanted to tell you that I carry our child."

The alien eyed her carefully as if he was looking through her. He used his eyesight, and he saw the insides of his mate and then saw a life growing in her womb. The alien was shocked but happy.

Yesele went to him and whispered. "

We need to find ways to escape. I don't want our child to go through the suffering we have. I want our child to have a happy life."

The alien eyed his mate. For he understood what she had told him. The feeling of protecting his offspring and mate was now his main priority. He had to get them out of this life, even if it killed him.

....

It had been three months, and Yesele felt that she was already full term with her pregnancy. It also surprised the scientists as they would check up on her progress. As the scientists did ultrasounds, everyone realized that the infant would be born any day. Yesele thought about what would happen to her once her child was born.

Would she live?

Would she die?

What was important to her was her child. She had to escape with the alien. She was in her room now, and she began to bang on the door. The guards opened the door and entered. "I-I'm sorry for the sudden outburst, but may I see the alien? I want to see him before the baby is born."

One of the guards shook his head. "We were ordered not to let you leave the room."

"Please, I don't know if I will live once I give birth. If there is the possibility that I may not live, at least give my last request. Ask the scientists to at least grant me this one last wish. I have done what they asked of me."

The two guards eyed one another. One of them got out his phone and began speaking. All waited, and the guard finished with his call. "I asked the higher-ups, and they agree with your request. You will only have an hour to meet with the alien. We will keep a close eye."

Yesele nodded; the two guards led her to the guarded room where she and the alien usually meet. Once inside the room, she sat on a chair, waiting for the alien.

The alien was forcibly let inside the room and then chained to the wall. Yesele went to him and hugged him.

The alien made a soft moan. She then put her lips by his ears. "We have to get out of here! The baby may be born any day! We can't have them get their hands on our child!"

The alien's eyes became wide open. Then, he began to struggle, making Yesele back away from him.

The guards saw what was happening and went towards the alien to try to control it. The alien was unchained from the wall; the alien used it as an opportunity. He gathered all his strength and pulled the chains, making the men lose their grip. Many flew mid-air when some landed on the floor or hit the wall cracking their skulls.

The alien then got a hold of his mate and began to run away from the room. The facility workers heard the alarms. The soldiers in the facility were gathering their weapons to get the alien back in its cage. The alien held onto Yesele and looked for the exit as quickly as possible. He found it and began to run towards it. The soldiers fired rubber bullets as well as sleep bullets. The alien dodged many of them.

Yesele was scared but hoped that the alien would help them escape. Suddenly, a pang of pain coarse in her womb and then her body. She then felt something drip from her private.

Her water broke. "No! Not now!" she cried.

The alien noticed his mate's distress. When he got distracted, he did not see when the guards fired a huge rubber tank-sized bullet at his face, making him lose balance and fall. He lost his grip on Yesele.

The alien was about to go to her, but the guards' shot tasers at him. The alien could not move. His body was filled with pain, and he watched as Yesele cried in pain. Then, the scientists stood before them.

"Nice try, but we are more prepared than you think. Now look, you both almost cost us the unborn test subject. It seems like she is ready to give birth. Take her to the birth room and keep the alien on a tight leash," said Dr. Logan.

The guards carried a screaming Yesele away from the alien. The alien was tied down as he yelped for his mate, who was about to give birth to their child.

Yesele was screaming in pain as the soldiers led her to a separate room. Once inside the room, female scientists tied her hands and legs to the bedposts. Never had she felt so much pain in her life. She felt that her insides were being torn apart. Sweat covered her entire body. Yet, the pain did not terrify her. It was the fact that she and the alien could not escape. They lost their chance to give their child a better chance of freedom.

There were many scientists present and a female doctor before her. "You are fully dilated; you can start pushing."

Yesele shook her head. "No! No! I don't want you to take my baby!"

The two scientists went to her. "You have no other choice, child. We will have this child born naturally or using other means."

The young woman cried; there was no other way. She felt another contraction, and the need to push was intense. There was no other option but to push. Yesele screamed in pain as she was not given an epidural to take the pain away.

Sweat dripped throughout her entire body.

"Good, I see the head!"

As Yesele pushed, she felt she was losing strength, and something poured out from her entrance. As she looked down, she realized that it was her blood. The scientists were doing nothing to stop the bleeding.

Yesele realized that they never wanted her to live; she was nothing more than a breeder to them. Yesele could feel the head of her baby coming out. However, she did not have enough strength left, and she felt the woman pulling her baby out by building more pressure on her womb.

Then...

Everyone present heard a cry. Her baby was born. With her strength, she lifted her head to see her baby. Her baby was covered in blood and was crying. Tears formed in her eyes.

"My...baby... boy...or girl...?"

The doctor cleaned the baby and handed the child to one of the scientists. "A boy. It seems he inherited your human side, but he also has some of the alien's attributes. You did your part," answered Dr. Antony.

Yesele could not stop looking at her baby, who was in the arms of a scientist.

"I...want...my baby..."

She felt more blood pouring out, making her weaker; her breathing was limited. "Let me hold...my baby...please..."

Tears formed.

The scientist ignored her and began to walk away to another part of the room. She extended her hand as if trying to reach her child. "My...baby..." She stopped breathing, and her arm fell and became motionless. A tear fell from her eyes.

Yesele was dead.

....

The alien heard his mate's screams of pain. It pained him that he was not there to help his mate. He was always alone and knew that his mate was forced to mate with him. They both grew to love and care for one another in the end. He was trapped and in bonds, for he could not move to save her.

He heard his mate's screams stop for what seemed like an eternity. There was silence; then, he listened to an infant's cry. That was when the alien knew that their child had been born. Happiness overwhelmed him, and he wanted to see his mate and child. Then, the doors opened; the alien saw the scientists walking out.

The alien saw the scientists holding a stretcher that was carrying a body. A hand was sticking out. His heart stopped; his mate was dead. He lost it, got out from his bonds, and went towards the scientists that were the cause of their suffering!

The other guards shot him down; he laid down on the floor with the pool of his blood. From the corner of his eye, he saw his child crying. He let out a painful groan, and his eyes went back to his mate's hand. With the strength he had left, he lifted his hand, trying to get his mate's hand.

He lost his strength; his hand fell to the ground. He did not move.

Both alien and Yesele were dead.

All that facility workers heard was the new life made from death.

Chapter 5

Since his birth, he was given no name, no human name. He was only called 'half-breed. The half-breed was experimented on by government officials ever since his birth. The child grew faster than any human child. Five months after his birth, he grew up into the height of a three years old human child and still had his alien traits, but would slowly dissipate as he grew older.

Ever since he was a child, the half-breed could climb and run faster than any human, even at his young age. He would eat any meat from any animal. When he was five years old, the half-breed would fight off animals twice his height and strength.

The scientists and officials were amazed by the half-breed's strength and experimented on him more as he grew older. About five years after his birth, he grew up into an adolescent form, his alien appearance disappeared, and he had a completely human appearance. During that time, he learned to transform into his alien form.

It was difficult to change because it was a painful process for him. The process made him feel like his skin was tearing, and his bones formed into different positions.

However, it made those around him lose their patience and try to force him to transform, which he would refuse. When they would use force, they would electrocute him, cut parts of his body, starve him, and dehydrate him.

The half-breed would almost die from time to time but would eventually give in to their demands.

Another form of experimentation would be fighting off other soldiers to see his combat skills; they were immense. He also would be trained to dodge bullets and other forms of weaponry. He would get injured or have parts of his body decapitated, but his body would heal and regenerate, not as fast as his pure-blooded alien father.

Years later, he became a full-grown adult. Even though he had extraordinary strength and gifts, he would not speak. He stood at six feet and three inches tall; his skin was light olive. His eyes were a dark gold color. He had a muscular build from all the pieces of training and fights he was forced to do. The half-breed held handsome features that made the most attractive male model shame. Like his father, his muscular body was filled with many scars that showed his abuse. He had short dark brown curly hair and a messy light beard.

There were times when he would refuse to communicate with the scientists and officials.

The half-breed often wondered if there was more to life than his captive facility whenever he had some free time. There were times when he desired to go to the outside world that his human mother was born into.

The scientists and government officials did not know that the half-breed was thinking of ways to escape prison.

Also, they didn't know that he would soon make his move.

....

Night befell the inhabitants of the facility. Many were going to their homes or going into the facility to work. For the half-breed, it was an everyday thing. He would look at the full-blooded humans who go on with their lives and work.

There was a part of him that was envious of them. They had the freedom that they were able to come and go from the facility as they wished. Never in his life had he been outside of the facility. He remembered when the scientists told him about his parentage. His father was a pure-bred alien, and his mother was human. When he was younger, he didn't understand the concept. However, as he grew older, he understood why the humans were so invested in knowing more about his abilities.

He is descended from beings that were of different worlds. The realization hit him that even though his mother and father were captured, they were once free. There were times when the half-breed wondered what life would have been like if his parents were alive.

Yet, the half-breed was alone.

He was sure that he wanted to be free as his parents once were. The need for freedom motivated him to study and learn all the strengths and weaknesses of the facility. He also knew every member of the facility by memory, their schedules, and much more.

Everything.

He had enough of being trapped throughout the years. He carefully planned his escape and today was the day that he would put all that he had learned into action.

....

Meanwhile, the two male scientists were walking through the halls. They were the ones that worked in the facility the longest and were in charge. Professor Antony, 55, and Professor Logan, 47, were in charge of the half-breed and were in charge of his parents. "It has been a while since we had the half-breed, and his powers are extraordinary," stated Antony as he took a sip of his coffee.

"Indeed, I am sure you received a message from the government, wanting to know more of the half-breed. I am sure they would want to use it for military purposes. However, I am concerned that it will interrupt our scholarly work. I wondered if we should bring females to mate with to study it more and sell them more. We-" Logan could not finish his comment when the alarm system went off.

"DANGER! DANGER! ESCAPE! ESCAPE!"

The workers of the facility were running everywhere. The guards were running towards the experiment room. Antony and Logan immediately went with the guards. When they arrived in the experiment room, they were met with thrown and decapitated bodies.

They saw the half-breed in his alien form growling as he was fighting the guards. He would dodge the bullets and slash anyone who would get in his way. The half-breed knew that more backup would arrive, and he wouldn't be able to fight them all off. He began to run, jump, and dodge everyone towards a closer exit.

Dr. Logan noticed this. "Stop him! He must not escape!"

The exit/entrance doors were closing. The half-breed ran faster. When the doors were about to close, he changed back to his human form and jumped out before the doors closed on him. Some guards were outside the facility, which began to shoot at him and the half-breed got hit, but it didn't faze him as he kept running. He then got to the fence and jumped over it.

Then, he went deeper into the woods. The half-breed felt the fresh air for the first time and enjoyed it. He felt small tears forming in his eyes. However, the half-breed kept running.

CHAPTER 6

That was when soldiers fired bullets.

One of the bullets hit a tree that the half-breed ran by. The guards saw him. "Don't let him escape! We must turn him in alive!" commanded one of the men. The drivers of the vehicles pushed on the pedals, making the trucks go faster. The dogs were in the vehicles, barking aggressively.

The half-breed looked behind him. The humans were catching up to him, but he was determined not to get captured. That was when he stopped for a moment and climbed up to a very tall tree. The half-breed hid within the leaves and branches. The darkness made it more difficult for the humans to try to get a closer glimpse and the half-breed used it to his advantage. The creature hid and breathed quietly, trying to regain his strength.

The vehicles stopped, and the lights were still turned on. The soldiers and their dogs got out of the vehicles as they held onto their weapons. They commanded their dogs to search, trying to get his scent.

The half-breed began to move among the trees, trying to keep quiet as possible. However, he stepped on a weak branch, and it fell in front of a dog.

The dog barked, jumping and looking up within the trees. He was seen.

"He's up there!" The guards got their weapons and began shooting up at the trees. The half-breed jumped to tree after tree. As he was about to go to another, a bullet hit his arm. He cringed in pain; it made him lose his footing, causing him to fall. His blood spurted out from his wound. One of the dogs got to him and bit him on the leg as he tried to get up.

The half-breed growled in pain as he felt his flesh torn by the dog. He made his right fingers grow into claws and killed the dog.

"There he is!" one of the soldiers took out a gun and shot a mere dart at him, which hit the half-breed in the shoulder. The half-breed refused to submit. Suddenly, his appearance began to change, his skin cracked open, and another form appeared. Tentacles formed out of his body and impaled all the soldiers and their dogs, killing them instantly.

Blood spurted out like rain.

The half-breed transformed into his human self and ran again into the woods. He ran farther and farther but then began to feel weaker and weaker as if he wanted to take a slumber.

Slowly, his eyes began to droop. As he ran through the darkness, he saw a light. A light that came from a place that was unfamiliar to him. He got closer and closer until darkness overcame him once again.

....

The half-breed began to feel his senses once again, even though he still felt weak. Slowly, he began to open his eyes, there was a bit of darkness, but his sight was getting better the more he opened them.

As he was opening his eyes, the half-breed felt different. He felt as if he was lying on something warm and comfortable.

Finally, the young man fully opened his eyes. The first thing he saw was the ceiling made of wood. He then looked both ways; a curtain had a flower pattern on his left side. A fireplace, a small wooden table with two chairs, a small kitchen with an old-looking stove, cabinets, refrigerator, and a sink were on his right. Far from the fireplace was a door leading to the bathroom and exit.

Confusion filled the creature. The half-breed tried to sit up but felt his body was too heavy even though he was slowly regaining strength. The half-breed was cautious but felt comfort, something he had never felt before. He had to sleep on the hard floor in the facility as he was treated worse than an animal. The feeling was new to him, and he felt that there was no danger at the moment. Slowly, he was closing his eyes again, but the door opened. He opened his eyes and turned his head towards the door.

Then, to his surprise, a young woman walked forward. To the half-breed, she was the most beautiful woman he had ever seen in his life. Sure, he had seen women in the facility, but they were not as beautiful as the one before him.

Her skin was pale but brought out her youth. She had long, wavy, light brunette hair with golden-red tips and light gray eyes. The young woman also had a thin but slight curvy figure; her face was very youthful with slightly pink blush cheeks. Her light pink lips were small and thin but made her seem more innocent. Many people who saw her would confuse her as an adolescent, even though she was an adult woman. She wore regular skinny blue jeans, a dark green t-shirt under a blue jean jacket.

She then put a bag on the table, looked at him, and smiled. "Oh, you're awake! Thank goodness! I saw you passed out in front of my house and you were injured! How are you feeling?" She went towards him, but the half-breed moved a bit far. The woman noticed and kept her distance. "I am not going to hurt you. I just wanted to make sure that you are well. Are you feeling a bit better?"

The half-breed just looked at her without responding.

"The name is Alesia. What's your name?"

He still did not answer and just eyed her.

As for Alesia, she stood feeling awkward with the silence. "Okay, maybe you don't want to talk or can't understand me. I will make some food for you." She was a bit thoughtful and did a hand sign. "Eat?"

To her surprise, the half-breed nodded.

Alesia smiled. "Great, I will make spaghetti if you don't mind." She went to the kitchen and unpacked the supplies she had. As she did so, the half-breed still looked at her.

He was speechless. Yet two words were stuck in his mind.

"Beautiful Alesia."

CHAPTER 7

lesia felt that she had to help him. What also made her curious was that his wounds slowly healed by themselves.

It scared her a bit, but she couldn't help being fascinated.

Alesia was done cooking the pasta and added the tomato sauce on top, along with the meatballs. Alesia got two plates, poured food on them, and then put the two plates on the table. Then, she got two loaves of bread and cups of fruit punch.

Everything was ready.

The half-breed sat up on the bed, intrigued by what the human female was doing. When the scent of food hit his nose, he felt his mouth salivate. Never had he smelled such good food before. The food he was fed in the facility was usually raw and hardly had any taste. There were times when the facility workers did not feed him at all.

Now he was free. The half-breed enjoyed the smell of freedom that he always longed for.

Alesia noticed him and smiled. "It is time to eat. Come on." She then motioned him to get off the bed, walk to the table, and sit on the chair. The young woman also motioned him the eating sign.

The half-breed, to his surprise, trusted her. He noticed that she did not try anything that would hurt him. He saw her make food, and she wanted him to eat. Slowly, he took off the covers and walked towards the small table. He sat on the farthest side; Alesia gave him a plate of food and his cup of juice. His eyes were wide open; the food looked delectable. He then saw Alesia giving him utensils, which confused him.

Alesia sat on the other side of the table and got the fork, rolled it to the spaghetti, and began to eat. The half-breed was fascinated. He got a hold of the fork and did what she did. It was a bit hard for him at first, but he got the hang of it with the third try. When he took his first bite, he felt like another world. The spaghetti was so delicious that he felt a tear form in his right eye. His thoughts were then interrupted.

"Hey there, are you okay? Have you ever eaten spaghetti before?"

The half-breed did not look at her and was slightly embarrassed; he kept eating. He then took a bite of bread and then a sip of juice.

He loved the taste of everything.

Alesia cleared his throat. "So, I saw you were injured. Were you in a fight?"

The half-breed did not answer.

"I can understand if you don't want to talk about it, but can you at least tell me your name?"

The half-breed stopped eating and slowly looked at Alesia. He looked confused.

"You do have a name, right?"

Name. It was foreign to him. He slowly shook his head.

Alesia's eyes became wide open. "You don't have a name? How is that possible!? Where are your parents?"

Still, he did not answer. "I guess you are not much of a chatterbox. Until you are ready to speak, how about I give you a name. I was thinking..." Alesia became thoughtful of thinking of a name. To her, men's names were a bit harder to choose. For female names, many were creative and had beautiful meanings. The half-breed eyed her with curiosity as he ate his last bite of bread.

"There are quite a few prevalent names, but I want to choose something different. Yet, there is one that I have always liked. How would you like your name to be Jedrek? What do you think?"

The half-breed moved his head as if trying to understand.

"I know you are not much of a talker, but I would like to know if you at least like the name. Take it as a new identity."

Then, something happened that shocked her.

"J-Jedrek." The half-breed spoke.

"Y-You actually spoke!"

He nodded. "I can speak. I always knew how."

Alesia was still in a state of shock. "Th-Then why didn't you speak!?"

"Cautious."

The young woman sat still; Alesia opened her mouth and raised an eyebrow. "You were cautious?"

"Yes."

"You could have spoken to me all this time?"

"Yes."

"You could have told me your name?"

"No."

"What do you mean?"

The half-breed looked at her. "I never had a name. I was never given one."

Alesia gasped. "You were never given a name!? Your parents never gave you one!? Why would they do such a thing!?"

"I never knew my parents; they both died when I was born."

Alesia was about to respond but then stopped herself. She was filled with confusion but also pity. The man before her never had a name and never knew his parents. "Did you have someone at least take care of you?"

The half-breed was hesitant to answer her. He did not want to tell her his true identity and all he went through. If he told her the truth, he was afraid she would fear him or turn him into the organization that kept him imprisoned all his life. "Not really. I had to survive on my own."

"Wow, I don't know how you are so calm about it. Have you ever on what to name yourself?"

He shook his head. "Not really; a name never came across my mind."

It was then silent between the two, but the half-breed broke the silence. "C-Could I have some more food? I haven't eaten in a while."

She nodded, got his plate, and served him more food. The half-breed ate with contentment, and Alesia just watched.

"Jedrek, I like it. That will be my name. I thank you for giving me a new identity."

The young woman slowly smiled. "After you are done, you can take a shower and go to sleep; I know you are exhausted." Alesia got up and went to wash dishes. Unknown to her, Jedrek kept on looking at her.

Chapter 8

After patrolling and looking for the half-breed who escaped, soldiers returned to the facility. Dr. Antony and Dr. Logan were enraged. The two men, including other scientists, were in a meeting room discussing what occurred.

"This is unbelievable! How could that half-breed escape this facility! I thought we had all the precautions to make sure to keep him here!" yelled Dr. Logan. He looked at the other scientists, who were afraid to speak.

"That is not even the worst of it, now that the half-breed escaped. It can be anywhere, and if its secret is revealed, it will know of it and this facility. I don't want the government to know of this. It will be the end of us!" exclaimed Dr. Logan.

The rest of the scientists discussed plans to retrieve the half-breed, but Dr. Antony and Logan did not have it. The two scientists dismissed the other scientists; the two were left alone.

"What are we going to do? If the government and other customers find out, we will lose everything we have worked hard for. If the wrong individuals find that half-breed, its existence will come to light. We can't let that happen."

Dr. Antony sat thoughtfully. "I doubt that it will make its identity known, it doesn't know of the world, and it will be cautious. I also believe that it will kill anyone that is a threat."

Dr. Logan sighed. "Let's hope you are right."

....

Meanwhile

Jedrek was lying on the bed, looking at the dark ceiling. He finished taking a shower about an hour ago. For him, it was the most relaxing thing he felt. He could take as long as he wanted, and the water was very warm.

At the moment, Alesia was the one taking a shower.

Jedrek knew that he needed rest, but Alesia intrigued him. She showed him so much kindness, and he wanted to learn more about her, how the humans lived, and so forth. He got off the bed and strolled to the bathroom, where Alesia was showering.

He quietly opened the door to see if she was available. As he caught the sight of her, he stilled. Jedrek saw Alesia, still in the shower, nude. He saw how the water flowed down her body like a waterfall, her eyes were closed, and there was a slight fog. However, he could still see parts of her body. She was thin, but her skin was light, her C-cup breast was in view, and her womanhood.

The half-breed had never seen a nude woman before. He did not know why, but he enjoyed the sight of her. It made him feel something he had never felt before. Suddenly, he felt funny beneath him. As Jedrek looked down, he saw that his penis had become erect.

He was shocked at what his entire being was feeling by the very sight of Alesia. Jedrek immediately went back to bed and breathed heavily, trying to calm himself down. His alien side made the feeling worse, as if it wanted him to take her now, but he did not want to. He breathed to himself, trying to sleep, thinking of anything else than Alesia's nude body.

....

It had been a week since Alesia found Jedrek. He enjoyed the time with Alesia. Alesia would still ask him about his past or present memories for the first couple of days.

He did not want to tell her the truth about what he was and what he had gone through. He liked the human woman very much that he did not want to ruin her likeness to him. A part of him feared that she would run away or inform the facility. However, Alesia stopped asking questions.

Since she intrigued him, Jedrek asked more about her. He learned that she lost her parents and lived with her elderly maternal grandmother in the woods when she was young. When her grandmother died, the house was left to Alesia. She loves nature and likes to draw. Currently, she works as a store clerk in a nearby village not far from her home.

He loved to listen to her talk, but he loved to see her smile most of all. She also informed him that she would let him stay as long as needed and gladly help him find his place.

He did not want to leave, but he just made her believe that he would move someday. At the moment, Jedrek was sweeping the floors while Alesia was outside and tending to her gardens.

As Jedrek was sweeping, he heard Alesia talking to some-one. It sounded like a male voice. He then looked out the window and saw Alesia talking to another man. Jedrek didn't notice it, but he squeezed the broom very hard.

Jedrek realized he felt jealous and competitive, especial-ly on his alien side. From what he knows about his alien heritage, male aliens are very ferocious when competing for females and will fight to the death. On the other hand, he was also half-human and knew he had to control himself. He dropped the broom and went outside to see the man's face. At his sudden arrival, both Alesia and the man looked at him.

Alesia smiled at Jedrek. "Jedrek, it's nice of you to get out of the house. I want to introduce you to one of my good friends and neighbors. This is Leo. Leo, this is Jedrek, the guy I talked to you about!"

Leo looked at Jedrek, and Jedrek did the same with Leo. Leo stood at 5'8 tall, with dark blondish hair that touched his ears with blue eyes. His skin was a little pale since he was more of a homebody with a couple of tattoos on his arms. The young man had a youthful look with a hint of rebellion. Leo also had an average body with little fat from his waist. He wore baggy blue jeans, dirty black shoes, a dark blue jean jacket with sleeves ripped off, and a black Metallica shirt that made him look like a typical rockstar. The young human male smiled and chuckled.

"So you are the famous Jedrek that Alesia can't stop talking about." He extended his hand towards the half-breed. "Pleased to meet you, dude."

Chapter 9

Alesia seemed to catch on, and he went to him. "Jedrek, he is trying to say hello; he wants you to get hold of his hand and shake it gently. It is a form of greeting."

The half-breed nodded, making sense of the situation. Now that he understood, but still didn't want to shake Leo's hand. His alien side was getting control of his actions. Jedrek felt that he shouldn't be blamed for something just in his nature. However, he wanted to leave a good impression of himself to Alesia. Slowly and unwillingly, he got a hold of Leo's hand and shook it but held it tightly than he should.

"You got a good grip." Leo and Jedrek got out of the handshake, and Leo massaged his hand a bit. Leo felt a bit of pain from the grip.

As for Jedrek, he mentally smirked.

Alesia then got between the two. "Hey Jedrek, Leo invited me to a lunch party with the other neighbors." She then looked at Leo. "Would it be okay if Jedrek came along? It would be a great opportunity for him to get to know the neighbors and be more outgoing?"

Leo nodded. "Sure thing. The party will be at noon at my house."

"Great. Would you like me to bring anything?"

"How about your famous shrimp cocktail and your beautiful self?"

Alesia blushed and playfully hit Leo on the shoulder. "We will see you there."

The two friends hugged one another, and Leo left. Jedrek watched him go. Even though the half-breed did not fully know Leo, he noticed how close Leo and Alesia were. He didn't like watching another male touching the female of his interest. His alien part growled mentally. His eyes glowed a dark red but dissipated when Alesia turned to him.

"Well, we need to get ready. I will start cooking so we can go."

Jedrek was sitting on the sofa, awaiting Alesia. She just finished making food for the little get-together. Alesia gave Jedrek some clothing and informed him that the clothing used to belong to her older brother, who lived in the city.

The half-breed wore a long-sleeved black buttoned shirt, blue jeans, and tennis shoes. He was a bit anxious about the upcoming activities; he had never been to a small party before. It would be interesting. On the other hand, he knew that Leo would be present and felt that Leo would try to be close with Alesia. He did not want that. Jedrek was new to these emotions, especially for a woman.

He took a glance at the door that led to Alesia's room. With his hearing, he could hear the young woman changing into a new set of clothing.

Strangely, it excited him. It also made his private excited. He closed his eyes and imagined Alesia changing and fully nude, trying to see her entire body. He did not realize that his penis was slowly getting erect as he was imagining.

Suddenly, the noise of a door opening made Jedrek open his eyes and realize that his penis was erect. He immediately noticed a pillow next to him and put it on his erection. Alesia walked out of her room wearing blue jeans, long black buckled boots, and a sleeveless white shirt with a light brown jacket. Her hair was made in a braid on the right side of her head.

Jedrek felt his lips apart. To him, Alesia looked magnificent.

"Are you ready to go?" she asked as she went to the kitchen to get the pot of food she had made.

The half-breed calmed his erect penis, stood, and merely nodded his head.

The two walked out of the house and began to walk out on a handmade walkway within the woods. The woods had a silent yet calm feeling to them. There were handmade poles of lights guiding their way. "So calm, right, Jedrek?"

Yes, quite soothing."

"There are other people that live within these woods. My neighbors and I like to live away from the city. It is so calm, peaceful, and less stressful."

Jedrek was a bit confused. "What's a city?"

Alesia raised her eyebrows. "You don't know?"

He shook his head. "It is a bit complicated."

"Well, a city is where a lot of people live. Many buildings are taller than these trees. There is much more to do in a city than here, but I prefer peace and quiet."

"Wow, sounds interesting."

She nodded. "I tend to live life slowly here. When one is in the city, they make their life go by at the drop of a hat. I'd rather take my time. I'd rather work to live than live to work."

Jedrek felt confused, and he was upset with himself. It also made him feel like an outcast and less human, even though he was half of it.

Alesia could not help but notice his seriousness. "Hey, brighten up! At least you will be out of your comfort zone! You also have me to help you become social!" She let out a giggle. About another twenty minutes after walking, the pair saw a couple of houses close to one another, a group of people together, with some tables, chairs, and fire beside them to keep them warm. "We will have a lovely time. Come on."

Jedrek followed her to the group of people. It will be the first time he will have actual conversations with other people.

CHAPTER 10

r. Antony and Logan were getting impatient and forced people in the facility to work longer until there was a sign of their experiment. They made sure to stress to the others to find the half-breed.

One of the technicians found something in the system that could lead to the half-breed as time progressed. The two scientists radioed many soldiers to go to the specific location that may lead to the one they were after. They were also ordered to kill anything and anyone that would stand in their way.

....

Jedrek sat among the other humans that he was not used to. He felt a bit off since he was never used to being so close to other humans in such a calm environment. However, he did not feel alone since Alesia was close to him.

She introduced him to her other neighbors, and they all looked to be friendly. At that moment, Jedrek looked down at his plate of food, and it had a hamburger, chips, and chicken, as Alesia described. He had to admit that the food was delicious. On the other hand, he couldn't help but feel annoyed that he was being stared at, especially by the other females.

Many tried to start a conversation, but Jedrek would give short answers or nod. He was not interested in them. He focused more on Alesia, who ate peacefully and spoke with others at the table. She laughed, smiled, as well as made jokes. He would take glances at her whenever he had the opportunity, but Leo came along. "Hey, Alesia." He looked at the half-breed. "Hey, Jedrek. I am happy that you both came along!"

Alesia giggled. "We are happy to be here. It feels like ages since we all did a party. I did miss everyone."

"I agree. I decided that we all should get together since we all work so hard."

Alesia took a bite of her hamburger. "So, how is your job at the office been?"

Jedrek watched intently at the two. He hated how Leo got to speak to Alesia so casually. What annoyed him even more, was that Alesia seemed to enjoy the conversation with Leo. Even though he met her not too long ago, he liked her.

Almost too much.

He wanted to stop them but felt that if he did, then it would cause too much tension, and he did not like that. As Jedrek was about to bite his food, a scent hit him. His eyes almost became wide as the smell was very familiar to him. He looked around to see where the smell was coming from. His eyes stopped on a man who had just arrived at the party. It was strange for Jedrek as he saw the man. He has never seen him before.

Jedrek fought off to let out a deep growl of anger. The scent was very familiar to one of the scientists from the facility. The unknown man greeted many people; Leo saw the man and went to greet him.

The scent brought him too many painful memories; he left the table. Alesia noticed and called out to Jedrek. "Hey, where are you going?"

"For a walk." With that, he went into the woods and began to walk. There were many trees and bushes. Even though it was dark, he could use his senses to know his surroundings. Walking helped him find comfort.

Jedrek looked up at the sky; it would be dark soon, and he closed his eyes. Even when Jedrek found some comfort, he still felt lonely. As Jedrek kept walking farther and farther, he stopped in his tracks.

He looked around as if trying to find something. Jedrek felt something was coming; it was not good news. He then smelled the air and felt his eyes glow.

His thoughts were interrupted when he saw a couple of trucks driving in his direction. He let out a vicious growl.

They found him.

Jedrek felt rage as he realized that he was outnumbered.

The soldiers noticed him and knew they had their target. One of them ordered the other men to stop the trucks, to give themselves space between themselves and their target. The soldiers came out of their vehicles, ready to fight.

Jedrek then focused on his enemies. He decided to stay and fight as he thought about Alesia. He didn't want her to get hurt or know the truth of what he was.

He stood his ground and was ready to fight.

The soldiers pointed to their machine guns; their sweat was apparent on their faces. "Come slowly, or we will be forced to fire!" one of them yelled at him.

"If you kill me, your worthless leaders can't do more experiments on me. If you want me, then come and get me, bastards!"

The soldiers were shocked. "It can talk!? I thought he couldn't!"

"I always knew, but I kept away from you all. I suggest that you all leave before I cut your heads off and eat them at my leisure."

The soldiers would not budge and kept their weapons pointed at their target. "Last chance, come quietly, or we will use force."

Jedrek's eyes were turning into a golden reptilian-like color. "Bring it." Then, one of the soldiers fired. Jedrek dodged the bullets and began to run toward them at inhumane speed. The other human soldiers fired, but their bullets missed.

Jedrek got behind one of them before the soldier and stabbed him on his back; his hand went through his chest. Blood spewed out. The others turned in shock and horror.

Jedrek immediately ran onto the trees to hide. The soldiers used flashlights on the machine guns to try to find him. He knew that he had to end them. Jedrek didn't want to use his other form but felt no other option. He then had tentacles coming out from his back, his body began to grow and make crunch-like sounds, and his face changed to a triangular-like shape. His skin color changed to dark blue color with reptile-like skin; his hands, arms, legs, and feet also had reptile-like features. However, he also had some human characteristics, such as his muscular build.

Jedrek jumped out from the large tree he was hiding in and stood before the soldiers in his alien form. The men could not move from the terror. Jedrek screeched and used his tentacles formed on his back and stabbed some of them in the face, heart, or stomachs.

More blood and body parts sputtered out. The others were about to shoot, but the half-breed threw the dead bodies towards them, making the soldiers miss. The others fell onto the ground with the dead weight on them. The soldiers accidentally dropped their weapons. Jedrek got a hold of them first and killed them.

Then, the half-breed went to them and slashed their heads off. His anger and hate towards them were too great. He didn't care if they were dead; all he wanted was to spill their blood. All the years of suffering made his blood boil.

He made sure that they were all dead in his alien form, and once he was satisfied, he immediately changed into his human form, naked.

Jedrek turned, and once he did, he stood still. His eyes became wide open. There he saw Alesia standing by a tree. She was hiding, and her body trembled uncontrollably.

Her face was filled with horror as she covered her lips and shook. Jedrek felt his body tremble in fear. He was afraid that Alesia would run away from him and not allow him to explain everything. "A-Alesia, I-" Before he could finish his sentence, Alesia fell to the ground. When he went by her side, he realized that she had fainted.

The half-breed got a hold of her, carried her bridal style, and walked home. He knew that he had a lot of explaining to do.

CHAPTER 11

Would she turn him in?

Would she be terrified of him?

Would she force him to leave?

So many questions went through his head; it made him even more nervous and afraid. He did not want to leave her. Jedrek wished to explain and let her understand that he wasn't entirely a monster. That all he wanted was freedom.

He made sure to go back and bury the dead soldiers, and as for the vehicles, he destroyed them, trying not to leave a trace. If the soldiers found him, then the facility was not too far away; he could be found at any moment. However, since the soldiers were dead, he knew that it would be difficult to track him. He had some time left.

Jedrek sat there waiting, and about thirty minutes later, he saw Alesia, moving and groaning. He didn't make a sound. The young woman opened her eyes and then sat up from the bed. She looked around; when her eyes led to Jedrek, her eyes became wide, and her back hit the wall.

Jedrek stood; Alesia screamed. "Y-You! Wh-What a-a-are y-y-y-you!?"

"Please calm yourself, Alesia! Believe me when I tell you that I will not and do not want to hurt you! I want the chance to explain!"

Alesia breathed heavily. "What are you!? How do I know that you are not lying!?"

"If I wanted to hurt you, I would have done so. I would have killed you if I did not want you to expose my secret. Please, let me explain, and you will know my truth. Please."

The scared young woman saw his face. She noticed the nervous look on his face but also his sincerity. She began to calm herself down but still kept her distance. "T-Talk."

Jedrek let out a sigh of relief and sat back down. "What you saw is one of my true identities. I am half-alien and half-human—basically a half-breed.

"A half-breed?"

"Yes, my father was an alien born on the Planet Mars, while my mother was a human."

Alesia put her arms around herself and cleared her throat. "R-Really? How was that even possible? How c-could that happen?"

Jedrek sighed and crossed his arms. It will all make sense if I tell you my parents' story. I will tell you how they met and how I came to be. It is going to be a while, but in the end, you will understand. It all started...."

Alesia listened to him as he told her everything; his parents, the lab, the scientists, childhood, and escape. It was silent between the two.

Jedrek sat silently, looking at the floor as he told the story. The scientists told him of his origin, and when they told him the story, they had a sense of amusement. Yet, the half-breed knew they were cruel and had no sympathy for him or his parents.

As for Alesia, she was aghast. She did not know what to say. There was so much to take in for such a short time. A part of her also did not know what to believe. She looked at Jedrek, who was looking down. It was as if he was ashamed to look at her in the face. Sorrow filled her heart.

Jedrek's parents went through so much suffering and died horrible deaths. Alesia could not fathom how Jedrek would have felt and what he had gone through. "Alesia..."

She was interrupted from her thoughts.

"I know it is hard to believe me. I will not blame you if you don't, but please believe me when I tell you that I would not lie."

Alesia bit her lower lip. "In a sense, you have."

Jedrek gave her his attention. "How?"

"When we first met, you lied to me. You never told me what you were."

The half-breed smiled. "You never asked if I was human or not. Technically, I didn't lie since you never asked." He then noticed Alesia raising an eyebrow and a slight pout; he thought it was adorable.

"So...those men you killed..."

"They worked for the facility and scientists that kept my parents and me prisoners. I escaped from them. I have no intention of going back."

Alesia began to pace back and forth. She began to think for a bit and felt hesitant to ask an inevitable question but felt she had to ask. "If they traced you, does that mean they are not far off?"

"It seems that way, but they keep their distance since they don't want to alarm other humans of my existence. I'm sorry, I should have told you, but I was afraid. I was afraid that you would fear me if I told you the truth."

Alesia felt sad for him. Jedrek went through so much; all he wanted was to live like an average human. "It is still hard for me to accept everything you told me. I am glad that I know who and what you are."

Jedrek felt relief, and he let out a sigh. He then stood from the bed and began to head to the door.

"Where are you going?" asked Alesia.

"I realized after today that I am putting you in danger. I don't want you to get hurt because of me. I need to leave." As Jedrek was about to open the door, he felt a grip on his left arm. He turned to see Alesia holding onto him.

It made his heart soar.

CHAPTER 12

"I-I can't let you go."

"What do you mean?" he asked in a soft tone.

The young woman was debating with herself on what to say. She let out a sigh. "I'm trying to say that I can't let you go through this alone."

Jedrek raised his eyebrows. "Even after I told you everything and knowing the risks, you still want to help me? Why? I am not worth risking your life for me."

"I want to help you, Jedrek. I can't explain it, but I have this sudden urge within myself to help you. It is not pity I feel; I care for you and your safety." She held his arm a bit tightly. "I don't want anything to happen to you."

"I can take care of myself, Alesia. I am a half-breed, as you previously saw."

Alesia sighed. "You think you can, but those scientists will not give up until they have you in their grasp! You are one against hundreds. Do you think you will be able to go against all of them? You need friends to help you!"

"Friends?" He shook his head. "I can't involve your friends."

"I will not let you go against them all alone! Your parents were probably not the only ones these sick creeps experimented on! This affects all of us. They will find others to experiment on even if something happens to you. Do you want the cycle to continue?"

Jedrek stilled. Cycle? Deep down, he knew that she was right. His parents had their lives taken away so he could be born. However, how many innocent people and beings were like his parents and himself. He had never thought about it before since he concentrated on survival.

He did not want to involve Alesia, but at the same time, he already did. She also brought up good points. He couldn't escape alone and did not want anyone else to suffer by their hands. Jedrek knew he had to stop them, even if it meant killing them. The half-breed looked at Alesia.

She had fear in her eyes but also determination. She wanted to help him. He couldn't help but feel happy and relieved. He knew it would be pointless to argue with her in the end. "Alright, you win."

Alesia smiled and let go of his arm. When he was about to speak again, she wrapped her arms around him and hugged him.

Jedrek did not know why, but he felt his face turning warm. He's never been hugged before. Slowly, Jedrek put his arms around her. He did not want to let go.

....

Meanwhile

There were a couple of soldiers in the woods, and one of them stopped when he saw the dead bodies. He called out to the others, and all surrounded the bodies. "He killed them all by himself. We have underestimated him," said one of the soldiers.

"What should we do?" asked the younger one.

"Take the bodies, for now. It is too dangerous to go after this thing. We don't know his full capabilities. We need to inform our superiors to see what they want us to do.

As moments went by, Dr. Logan and Antony were feeling annoyed. They and four other scientists were in the meeting room with large projectors of government officials. Some way or another, they found out about the half-breed's escape; they were not happy.

"I can't believe the alien escaped under your charge, Dr. Logan and Dr. Antony. We chose you to take charge of this experiment, and now this happens." It was the General of the United Army that spoke out. He then shook his head. "My colleagues and I should have learned from your previous mistake when you had to kill the pure-blooded alien."

"Now that this half-breed escaped, it can lead to cat-astrophic events! Society will learn of it; it can lead to much-unwanted attention!" said a female government offi-cial. "So, what is the update for its capture?" she asked.

"We are doing everything in our power to bring it back. We sent out reinforcements and found its location," answered Dr. Antony.

Dr. Logan then stepped forward. "The half-breed has not gotten far; our location is far from any city. There is nothing to worry about. We assure you that we will capture this alien."

The other officials were quiet. The General of the U.S mili-tary huffed. "You will have a week to contain this thing. If you don't recapture it, you will lose more than your career. We had enough of all of your incompetence." Then, all the projectors turned off. The two lead scientists and the others were silent. Many of the underlings were worried.

"It is a threat; we might lose our lives because of this!" a middle-aged female scientist said.

Another male scientist eyed their leaders. "So what now? We haven't heard from the men we sent out."

Dr. Antony rolled his eyes. "You all worry about something so trivial, go on and leave us. I don't want my headache to worsen."

The scientists did as they were told, leaving the two alone. Dr. Logan sat in his seat. "What a mess. I cannot believe that the half-breed would escape."

Dr. Antony also sat. "Indeed, but I will admit that I am impressed, its father could not entirely escape, but its progeny did. It inherited human intelligence. We were right to have the woman and the alien mate.

Suddenly, there was a knock on the door, and a soldier entered.

The two scientists eyed the commander and immediately knew what he was about to say. "I take it that you did not find the half-breed," said Dr. Logan.

"Our men found it, but the freak killed them. I am sure it used its alien form to do so. I had to make my men retreat since we didn't know what we were fully up against. I also did not want to lose more manpower."

"Our little experiment is intelligent and seems to know how to fight." Dr. Antony smirked. "You and your men rest up; tomorrow, we will have a meeting and tell you everything we gathered on it."

The commander nodded and left the room.

"You are too relaxed for your own good, Antony."

"Calm yourself, Logan. The half-breed has not gone far. I want drones to be sent throughout the forest to see if there are any inhabitants."

Antony's eyes lit up. "What are you planning?"

"There are always fools that live or build homes in the forest for their use. This forest, in particular, is vast and can be easy to get lost in. I have a hunch that the half-breed will not be alone."

CHAPTER 13

At the same time, he did not want to put her in danger, but she was stubborn. A scent hit him as he lay on the bed, and it smelled delicious. Jedrek got off the bed. When he went to the kitchen, Alesia was already awake and dressed. She was cooking breakfast.

"Good morning Alesia."

She turned and smiled. "Morning, Mr. Alien. I hope you slept well."

"Uh, quite well. What's with the name?"

"Yeah, a little nickname. Nicknames are given to others as a way to show affection." Alesia paused for a moment. "Would you rather me stop?"

He shook his head. "No, it's quite alright. What is that? It smells good."

"Pancakes, sausage, and eggs. Take a shower. After we are done eating, we will meet with Leo."

Jedrek raised an eyebrow. "Leo?"

"Yeah, remember that guy from the party?"

Jedrek finally remembered and nodded. "Okay, I will shower." He went to the bathroom and, with the help of Alesia, turned on the shower, and he was left alone. He undressed and got in the shower; the warm water hit his body. He was washed with cold water in the facility, sometimes with force. This new feeling was something he enjoyed. Jedrek couldn't stop thinking that he and Alesia visited Leo today. He let out a slight growl.

When he finished, he got a towel and went out of the bathroom, and when he opened it, Alesia stopped in her tracks. He noticed a blush on her face. "I-I was about to knock on the door to give you fresh clothes!"

"Oh, thank you." He let go of the towel to get a hold of his new clothing, but the towel fell, exposing his lower body and private part.

Alesia squealed and covered her eyes. "J-Jedrek! C-Cover yourself and go change!" She walked away immediately.

Jedrek felt a little confused about why she acted in a certain way. He couldn't help but let out a slight smirk when he looked down. "Oh, I see now. Human females get a little excited to see a man's penis. Yet, she did look embarrassed. Who knows, maybe she is hiding her excitement." Jedrek got dressed in dark blue Levi jeans and a long-sleeved dark blue shirt, and he undid a few buttons to show off his chest. He went to the kitchen, where Alesia served the plates.

She looked up, and Jedrek smiled innocently. "I apologize. I am not used to having showers or using towels."

"I-It's okay. Let's eat up so we can go."

Both sat and began to eat their food. It was quiet between them, but Jedrek decided not to speak much, for he knew that Alesia was still processing everything that happened the previous night and for her to see how much of a male he was.

....

Jedrek felt like a child at the moment. He and Alesia were walking toward Leo's house. He tried to calm himself. They finally reached Leo's house, and Alesia knocked on the door. Both waited, and the door opened. Leo stood in gray sweats, a plain white t-shirt, and his hair in disarray. It looked as if he barely woke up.

"Morning, Alesia. I'm surprised that you are up this early."

Alesia giggled as she shook her head. "This is the time that people are already awake. You are just lazy."

Leo chuckled and noticed Jedrek standing from afar. "Hey, is that your new friend. Jackson, right?"

Jedrek felt annoyed.

"No, his name is Jedrek. I can't believe you already forgot his name. Anyway, we came here because we have something important to discuss."

Leo noticed how Alesia's face became serious. "Come in." Jedrek and Alesia entered. Jedrek noticed how a bit messy

Leo's house was. There was so much paperwork, books, and some uncleaned dishes.

"Sorry for the mess. I have been busy with the new book I am writing."

"Book?" asked Jedrek.

"Yeah, I don't know if Alesia told you, but I am a conspiracy theorist and tend to research the government and their secrets."

Jedrek couldn't help but be amused but decided not to say anything further. Alesia cleared her throat. "Anyway, there is something serious we need to talk about. Also, we do need your help."

"What is it?"

"I came to you since you are quite obsessed with conspiracy theories, even though many were boring."

Leo acted hurt, but he let her continue.

"Leo, have you ever researched aliens?"

This captured his interest, although he was surprised that she would ask him about such a thing. "Of course. Why?"

Alesia took a deep breath. "What if I said that the government hiding aliens is true?"

"Woah, what are you trying to get at?"

"That an alien has been among us."

Leo was confused. "What?"

Jedrek rolled his eyes. "What she is trying to say is that I am a half-breed. I am half-human and half-alien."

It was silent between all the three. Alesia and Jedrek awaited for Leo to respond. Then, Leo's body began to shake, and
to their surprise, Leo laughed.

Alesia and Jedrek watched as Leo laughed aloud. Alesia
sighed as she shook her head. Jedrek raised an eyebrow in
amusement. For what seemed like forever, Leo's laughs died
down. "Nice, you're quite funny! All of a sudden, you are saying
that you are half-alien!"

"You're saying you are this so-called conspiracy theorist
who believes in government secrets."

The two men glared at one another. Even when Jedrek first
met him, he knew it was within his instincts that he did not
like Leo, but now, he loathed him even more. At the same time,
he knew that she shouldn't entirely blame him. They would
be in disbelief if Jedrek and Alesia told any other human his
secret.

"Leo, I am very serious. Jedrek is half-alien. Remember the
day of the party that I went to find him? I found him on
his alien form, and he was fighting off soldiers of a secret
organization."

Leo shook his head. "You know what I think? This guy is
completely nuts. I can tell that you haven't known him for
very long."

Jedrek was getting irked. "I agree; I don't know why she
would even be friends with a so-called conspiracy theorist in
the first place. You are even crazier than I am, although some

things are hidden from you, humans. As for me, on the other hand, my truth has always existed."

"Alright, you two, that is enough. Leo, what I am telling you is the truth. You know I have been more skeptical of what you tell me."

"What, you mean that you were lying to me this entire time?"

The young sighed in annoyance. "Anyway, I am the type of person who would want proof of the unexplained; yesterday, Jedrek proved to me that aliens are real." As Alesia was about to continue, she was interrupted by Jedrek.

"Alesia, this human is stubborn to the core; he will not believe us until we show him proof." He stood and began to undress.

Alesia squealed. "What are you doing!?"

Jedrek mentally smirked. "I can't have the clothes be ruined. Besides, I wouldn't want to wear his clothes." As Alesia covered her eyes, Leo flinched and saw Jedrek fully in the nude, and then he saw it.

Leo's eyes were wide, and a sense of jealousy overflowed him.

"No way in hell can it be that huge,"

he said.

Then, Jedrek's body began to make cracking sounds, and his skin color and appearance changed. Leo's eyes and mouth became more expansive as he saw Jedrek's body growing and changing. Jedrek's human form was no more, and he was now in his alien form.

CHAPTER 14

"WH-WH-WHAT THE F-F-F...!!" Jedrek growled. Alesia gathered her courage and went next to him. "He believes you now. You can change back." He nodded, and he slowly began to change into his human form.

Jedrek was now fully human. "Now, do you believe me, human?" He got his clothing and began to change.

Alesia stepped forward before Leo. "We came to you because you are an expert in your field, and we need your help. We need your help to gather allies to help Jedrek be free."

Leo was still breathing heavily, trying to cope with what he had just witnessed. Sure, he did believe that the government was hiding secrets from the public eye. He also believed in life outside of earth, but he now witnessed a man turning into an alien. Leo almost found it hard to believe that Jedrek is a half-alien.

So many questions went through his head.

"So, will you help us?"

Leo goes out of his thoughts. "Wh-What?"

"I asked if you would help us?" asked Alesia.

Leo got up and then sat back on his sofa. "T-This is too much to take, Alesia. I just saw this dude turning into an alien, and you want me to help hide him from the government!? This is crazy!"

Jedrek merely rolled his eyes. "You were thought of being crazy when you believed in many conspiracies." He then looked at Alesia. "How can this lunatic help me? I can tell that he is scared as it is." Jedrek sighed and got a hold of Alesia's left hand. "As I said, I don't want you or others to get involved."

Alesia looked at Jedrek and then at Leo. "Please, Leo, Jedrek has been through so much when he lived at the government facility. His parents suffered also. His dad was an alien found on Mars and was experimented on. His mother grew up in the foster care system all her life and was chosen to breed with Jedrek's alien father. Both are dead, and now Jedrek escaped, hoping to live a normal life."

Leo eyed Jedrek, and Jedrek did the same. "If that is the case and he did escape, then that means this so-called facility is not far from here, which means he already put us in danger."

Jedrek flinched. "I told Alesia that I would rather face this alone, but she is adamant that she wants to help. She can be stubborn."

Leo then glanced at Alesia, who looked at him pleadingly. He let out a long sigh. "Fine, I'll do it. This is a great opportunity to shed some light about the government."

"You should do no such thing. If people discover my existence, then I will have no peace; other governments and black markets will try to come after me."

"Jedrek has a point, Leo. Like the rest of us, I want Jedrek to be safe and live a normal life. Is that something you would want if you were in his situation?"

It was silent between the three. Leo massaged his head. "Okay, I will help, but you can't stay in your home, Alesia. As I said before, we are all in danger since Jedrek is an important asset to the government. I have a buddy in the military who has a huge distrust of the government. I will call him up so you both can meet him."

"Thank you, Leo! Thank you!" Alesia hugged him.

Jedrek bit his lower lip.

"Well, we gotta go. Call when your buddy comes by."

The two left Leo's house. "Are you sure you can trust him?"

"Yes, Leo may not look like it, but he can help us. Anyway, I want to take you out."

"Out?"

Alesia smiled. "Yeah, I want to show you how to be human!"

CHAPTER 15

Jedrek was looking outside the window as Alesia was driving her car. They passed the woods and now were on the open road. Jedrek felt the breeze hit his face, and he enjoyed the feeling.

Alesia would take glances at him and smile. She was happy that Jedrek was at peace and enjoying the taste of freedom.

"So, you said that we are going to a town. Is that where there are many people?"

"Yup, there are people, animals, stores, and other things. I want to tell you that you can't tell anyone what you are. Some people may think you're crazy or will be suspicious of you, resulting in unwanted attention."

Jedrek nodded. "Understandable; I want to have at least some freedom."

Another hour went by, and they both made it to the nearest town. Jedrek was in awe at its beauty: the people, the buildings, everything. He always dreamed of seeing it, and now it has become a reality. "I have never seen a place so beautiful."

"There are other places that are bigger and more beautiful than this. There are so many things to explore."

"Still, no matter if it is big or small, it would still amaze me."

Alesia then parked her car on the side of a street, and they both got out of the car. Jedrek saw many people in shops, restaurants, or walking their dogs. He felt as if he was in heaven. He then felt Alesia's hand on his shoulder. "Come on, let's have a quick bite to eat."

She then led him to a small ice cream store, and Jedrek saw many flavors he could smell using his intense nose. He liked the smell of many, but there were some that he was not too fond of. Alesia ordered a double scoop of mint chocolate chip and rocky road. Jedrek looked and smelled the scents and made his decision. He saw the names of each of the flavors. "I-I would like cookies and cream and the recess ice cream."

The owner served Jedrek's ice cream to him, and Alesia paid for them using her credit card. She then led them to a table outside the shop, and both began to eat their ice cream.

Jedrek felt the cold and delicious flavors of the ice cream, and never in his life had he ever tasted something so sweet.

Alesia watched as he ate his ice cream while savoring the moment. She thought it was an adorable sight to see. She wanted him to give and show him more freedom. Alesia wanted him to be happy, and she was going to do everything in her power to do so and to help him entirely escape those scientists.

The two finished their ice cream, and Alesia took Jedrek to other places such as the library, clothing, and food stores. However, they couldn't go to the pet shop because many animals either growled, barked, or were out of control. The animals had a sense that Jedrek was not fully human.

However, Jedrek was having a lot of fun. Alesia then looked at the theater and suggested they watch a movie. The theater was known to show old movies from time to time, and Alesia looked at the listing. "Hey, they're showing Gladiator. Let's watch it."

"Gladiator?"

Alesia smiled. "You'll see." She got the tickets and paid for them, and both went inside the theater. Jedrek couldn't help but feel amazed at how beautiful the theater was and how comfortable it felt. Alesia then took him to one of the theater rooms, and they both sat in the middle rows. To their luck, they were the only ones.

Moments later, the movie began, and the two watched with eagerness. Gladiator was one of her favorite movies, and she could only hope that Jedrek would like it. During the movie, she would look at Jedrek, who was engrossed in the film and seemed to enjoy watching the movie.

On the part where Commodus and Maximus were fighting, Jedrek was filled with anticipation. Both died. One died in shame, while the other died with his vengeance.

The movie finished, and the two got out of the theater. "So, did you enjoy the movie?"

"Yes, that was my very first movie."

"Who was your favorite character?"

"Maximus, of course, but I couldn't help but feel pity for Commodus."

Alesia raised an eyebrow. "Why?"

"Well, Commodus only wanted to prove himself and get his father's recognition. True, there is no excuse for him to kill his father. However, Marcus also admitted that he failed as a father. His failure was his and his own son's downfall."

The young woman nodded. "When you put it that way, it makes sense, but I still don't like the guy."

Jedrek chuckled, and they both decided to sit on a bench to look at the people and watch the sun slowly setting down. "I want to thank you for showing more of the outside world. Also, for helping me enjoy my freedom."

Alesia smiled. "You're welcome; I wish I could take you to more places."

"No worries, this was sufficient, especially being born in captivity." The two sat silently. Slowly Jedrek put his arm behind Alesia, looking as if they were a couple. Alesia felt his hand on her neck and felt her face turn warm.

The two looked at one another, and their eyes were on one another. As they eyed one another, they looked like they were in a trance. Slowly, their faces were getting closer to one another, and Alesia's phone rang when their lips were close to touching. Both cleared their throats, and Alesia answered the phone.

Jedrek felt annoyed that their moment was interrupted.

Alesia finished with the phone call. "It was Leo; his buddy is at his house and wants to meet us."

CHAPTER 16

Alesia and Jedrek drove away from the small town. The two were quiet along the way. Jedrek was angry that his time with Alesia was interrupted.

On the other hand, he should have expected this. There are other things at hand, and know that everything lasts forever. They got to the woods and the road leading to Leo's home. Once they got there, the two noticed a jeep parked close to Leo's house. Alesia parked her car, and the two got out.

"Let's see if this guy can help."

They got to the house, and Alesia knocked on the door.

Leo immediately opened the door and motioned them to enter. Once inside, the two saw a tall man with a muscular build, dark short blonde hair tied, blue eyes, and a slight dark blonde beard. His face was youthful, but the beard made the man look more masculine and older. The unknown man also was 5'7 tall. He wore an Army dark green shirt with black Levi jeans; with black shoes.

Jedrek did not know why, but he felt jealous of the man. He had to admit that the man was very good looking and Jedrek felt threatened by that. However, the more Jedrek looked at him, he thought the man looked familiar. "Was this man in the party?"

"Yeah, Alesia, Jedrek, this is my buddy, Fred. Fred, they are Alesia and Jedrek. Jedrek is the guy I was telling you about."

Fred walked forwards and shook Alesia's hand. Then, he went to Jedrek. The two men eyed one another. Fred extended his hand, and Jedrek glared at him; he smelled Fred's scent and growled. "Your scent, it reminds me of that place!"

Fred saw Jedrek's eyes change and slowly backed away, putting his hands up midway.

"Jedrek, please calm yourself!" said Alesia.

"So it's true," said Fred. "I guess he never changed. You were part of his experiments."

"What are you talking about?" asked Leo.

Fred sighed. "I knew someone who worked in the facility."

Alesia and Leo were shocked, except Jedrek. He still glared at Fred and growled. Fred sighed. "Look, man. I'm not your enemy. I had to see you myself when Leo told me about you."

"Wait a minute; you had an idea that a facility was here? Why didn't you say anything to me?" asked Leo.

"I didn't want you to poke your nose in dangerous situations. Knowing you, you would have tried to find the facility, which is not far from here." Fred focused on Jedrek. "Anyway, I'm amazed that you escaped."

Jedrek rolled his eyes. "I had to plan for so many years to try to escape. Having my freedom was my main motivation."

Fred nodded. "You are pretty smart. I wish I were when I joined the military. I thought I was fighting for this country's freedom and wanted to please my dad, for he wanted me to work with him. However, I saw things that no one should see and realized we are being used by the powerful. I found out some secrets that made me quit the military. My old man was pissed, and we never spoke again."

"Oh, I'm sorry," said Alesia.

"Don't be. I am happy that I am thinking and following what I want."

"So, you knew someone who used to work for the facility?" asked Alesia.

Fred nodded. "Yeah, but first, I know some things about it." He eyed Jedrek. "I need you to tell me more about yourself and the facility."

Jedrek raised an eyebrow. "Why?"

"Because there is a 100% chance we will face them."

....

When Jedrek explained the facility to everyone, all were thoughtful and silent. Fred sat with his hands under his chin. He nodded. "Thanks for the information. Now that I know more of its structure and resources, we have a better idea of what we are fighting against."

"Woah, are you saying that we are going to fight them? Fred, we are a bunch of nobodies compared to that organization! They can kill us off easily!" said Leo.

Fred sighed. "They will kill us all since we know their secret and of Jedrek's existence. These people would silence anyone to keep their existence secret."

"That is why I wanted to leave Alesia. I did not want to put her in danger."

Leo glared at him. "Only Alesia, you both got us involved in this!" He then eyed Alesia. "You should let him leave!"

"Shut it, Leo! I am not going to leave Jedrek alone! You were always talking about your conspiracy theories about the government. Talking like you are high and mighty! I can't believe that you're so selfish! That was one of the reasons why I rejected you!"

Jedrek flinched.

"So he was interested in Alesia,"

he thought to himself.

Leo cleared his throat as Fred stood up from his seat. "I will talk with some of my buddies from the military. Many of them hate the government. We can always help a brother in need."

"Thank you," said Jedrek.

"It is no problem, and I would do anything to help." Fred showed himself out of Leo's house. Alesia glared at Leo and motioned Jedrek to follow her, which he did. They both went back to Alesia's house and the living room.

Alesia massaged the sides of her head, and Jedrek knew she was going through a lot.

"I'm sorry."

"Don't be. It is a lot to take in, but this is what I chose, and I am sticking to it. The bright side is that we are not alone."

Jedrek smiled. "Yeah."

"By the way, I wanted to ask you something."

Jedrek nodded for her to continue.

"When Fred came, you said you recognized his scent from the facility. How is that possible?"

He was silent for a bit. "His scent smelled of another. A person I knew from the facility."

Alesia gasped. "What are you trying to say?"

Jedrek took a deep breath and calmed himself. "I didn't want to say anything because I did not want to make the situation worse than it already is, but with his scent, and if I am correct, he is related to one of the scientists that experimented on me and my parents. He may be the son of Dr. Antony."

Chapter 17

No one could deny what he was. Fred and his soldier friends agreed to help Jedrek against all those in the facility. It was decided that the participants would return by the end of the week for proper training.

As for Leo, he kept his distance and decided not to fight. However, since he knew much about technology, he would be their eyes, which everyone agreed with.

Alesia and Jedrek were outside the house, waiting for everyone. The two sat outside the home bench, waiting for the arrivals. "What time do you think they will arrive?" asked Jedrek.

"Soon, don't worry, they will come."

Alesia noticed how thoughtful Jedrek became, and she put a hand over his. "Don't worry. Everyone agreed to help you out. You know that those who want to help you hate the government and what it has become. They once believed in them, but after fighting for them, they learned that their leaders never cared in the end."

"The ones running the facility are dangerous and trained by the best. They also have weapons as well as technology that is too advanced."

"You have observed them for so many years. You know their strengths and their weakness. You know the way in and out."

Jedrek sighed. "You always find a positive side to everything."

Alesia smiled.

He then put his other hand over hers. "I don't want you in this fight." Alesia was about to speak out, but she was stopped. "You have no experience in fighting, and you can easily be killed. I want you to leave this place."

The young woman was shocked. "I'm not going to do that! Are you insane! I told you that I want to help you no matter what!"

"No buts. I am going to tell Leo to take you elsewhere."

Alesia stood up. Anger was apparent on her face. "You will not tell me what I can and can't do, Jedrek! Is it because I am a woman!? You think I'm weak!?"

Jedrek sighed. "No, it's not like that."

"Then what then!? Why can't I fight!?"

Jedrek stood up and got a hold of her shoulders. "It's because I don't want to lose you! I don't want you to get hurt or get killed! The mere thought of that will destroy me!"

Alesia's eyes were wide open, and without any warning, Jedrek got a hold of the back of her head and pulled her to his face. His lips were on hers. Jedrek's other arm was around her waist, making her body closer to his. She was in shock and could not move. His lips were warm, and his kiss was passionate. Slowly, her hands were on his back.

Alesia kissed back.

However, they did not know that something was watching their every move from afar.

Alesia and Jedrek broke away from the kiss; their eyes were on one another. She cleared her throat. "I um...well....I...."

"You feel the same way I do."

She blushed as she looked away but felt his fingers under her chin, making her look at him. "Don't look away. I know it was very soon, but what I did just now is my truth. You don't have to answer immediately, but I was hoping you could think about it. No matter what you answer, I will respect it. However, my feelings for you will never change."

Alesia couldn't help but blush. As she was about to speak, noises of vehicles were coming their way. They saw cars and some trucks. Fred was the first one out as the vehicles were parked, and other men and women came out with their weapons.

"Hey, you guys, we made it. We brought weapons just in case we needed them and also to get your input about the weapons the soldiers in the facility have."

Jedrek nodded. Alesia walked forward. "Please come inside; we have a lot to talk about."

....

In the facility, Dr. Antony and Dr. Logan looked at the footage from one of the many drones they had sent to find their specimen.

"Who would have thought that our experiment has found himself a female. I wonder if he mated with her yet," said Logan as he drank a cup of coffee.

"I doubt it. If they barely kissed, they haven't gone through that stage yet. He also seems to be gathering allies." Antony was looking at the footage, especially one man in particular.

Logan noticed. "It seems that your son is getting involved. What a small world this is. When was the last time that you saw your son?"

"Long ago, when I divorced his mother. I once brought him here when he was a child. I was hoping he would follow in my footsteps, but I realized he was soft and would never follow me in my place. That is why I left."

"You were always cold-blooded, but your son served in the military, from what I hear. A bit of an accomplishment."

Antony chuckled. "That boy does not know how to accomplish things, and now he is putting his nose where it doesn't belong."

Logan ate a piece of a doughnut. "What happens if he tries to fight us?"

"Then, he dies, as well as the other soldiers. We must keep this facility a secret. However." Antony looked at the image of Alesia. "We need to keep the girl alive."

"I see, so that is your plan, but when should we strike?"

Antony smirked as he stood up from his seat. "When they are at their most vulnerable. She is the key to getting back our little half-breed."

CHAPTER 18

Everyone was situated within the house. Jedrek, Fred, and Alesia stood before the group.

Jedrek then stepped forward. "I have been in the facility since I was born. The main reason for my birth is to be experimented with, to see my abilities. My father was an alien from another planet. He, too, was experimented on. The scientists and the government wanted my father and mother to procreate to see how a half-breed would work from a pure-bred alien."

"Why? What is their purpose?" asked a female soldier.

"They wanted to make half-breed soldiers to control. The government wants complete order over the human population. Also, they want half-breed soldiers to carry out assassinations to kill those who are a threat to their power."

The soldiers mumbled to one another. Alesia put her arms around herself. She couldn't believe what she was hearing, but at the same time, it was understandable. Times have changed in politics; there is much more corruption and greed for power.

Humans can be fickle and cruel creatures.

"However, my father was killed when trying to save my mother. They wanted to use him to mate with other females to procreate more half-breeds, but their plan failed. Now they were relying on me to help procreate. However, they don't know what would happen if I procreate."

"What do you mean?" asked Fred.

Jedrek sighed. "There might be a possibility that if I did produce offspring, they would inherit alien genetics, but the DNA can become minimum."

"However, it is not for certain, right?" asked Fred.

Jedrek nodded. "Now, since you all want to help stop this organization, I will tell you everything I have witnessed and what I know. I will also personally train you. However, we must prepare in secret, for the facility is not too far. I am sure they have spies around. Does anyone happen to know a good place to train?"

Another soldier stood up. "I own my gym. We all can train there."

"Perfect, please give us the directions. Tomorrow I will begin explaining everything and begin the first phase of training."

Everyone nodded, and the soldier texted everyone the address, and everyone was set. Jedrek and Alesia knew this was the beginning of a war, and no one knew the outcome.

....

Tomorrow would be the day when everyone would be starting their training. Everyone left; he and Alesia were at home. Alesia ordered a pizza for them to eat, and he enjoyed the food immensely. The two were done, and now we're both in the living room by the fireplace.

"I thank you for everything you do for me, Alesia."

"I am happy to help, Jedrek. It's the least I can do."

Jedrek was silent for a bit. "I don't want you to fight."

Alesia rolled her eyes. "Not this again. I told you that I had already made up my mind. No matter what, I will join the fight."

"No, you won't. I let you help me, but that's about it. You can stay with Leo."

The young woman let out a huff. "I will not do that! I want to fight! Do you think I can't because I am a woman? There were soldiers here that were women."

He shook his head. "It's not because of that; you have no experience taking a human life. Those soldiers and I were trained to kill to survive; you have to have a gift for killing with no remorse. You would not be able to live with yourself if you killed someone. I know; I can feel it. Please believe what I tell you. I don't want you to hate yourself."

It was silent between the two of them. Alesia was shocked that he would tell her such a thing, but at the same time, she knew that he was right. "Okay...fine. I will stay with Leo. But promise me something."

"Yes?"

"Come back alive."

Jedrek gave her a soft smile. He knew that the scientists and their men were influential, and many would die. He did not want to lie to her. Jedrek would do anything if it meant that she lived. He went closer to her and put his hand over hers. "You are my motivation."

Alesia felt her eyes becoming watery, and she then put both her hands on his face and pulled him to her face. Her lips touched his, surprising Jedrek. Her lips were cool and soft; it made him shiver with anticipation. He then returned the kiss; his tongue touched hers. The two tried to fight for dominance, but Jedrek overcame her. They then separated from the kiss, trying to catch their breath.

The young woman noticed his eyes change color. Alesia touched Jedrek's face and kissed him again, but her lips trailed down from his lips to his neck. Her hands then began to touch his body. Jedrek was never handled like this before, but he couldn't deny that it made him feel excited. He felt his member becoming erect, and his pants blocked his erection. Alesia noticed and gave out a small gasp. She saw that his erection tried to rip through his pants.

"I-I'm sorry, I-" Jedrek was interrupted when Alesia slowly put her hand over his bulge and massaged it. Jedrek was surprised by her actions. Jedrek let out a low growl. Then, Alesia began to undo the zipper from his pants, freeing his member. Her eyes became wide open. His member ripped through his boxers.

Alesia blushed as she saw Jedrek eyeing her as if she was his prey. He grabbed her right hand and put it on his erection. She knew what Jedrek wanted. She moved her hand up and down, and Jedrek arched his head back; he growled in pleasure. Then, he felt something wet, and when he looked, Alesia had his member in her mouth. His eyes became wide. Jedrek couldn't deny that he felt good. He put his hand on her head and let Alesia pleasure him.

He moved his waist with her rhythm. Moments later, Alesia took his member out of her mouth and gave out small pants. "Sorry, I didn't know what came over me."

Jedrek smirked. "There is more to you than meets the eye. Have you done this before?"

She blushed. "Once, with my first boyfriend. It didn't work out."

Deep down, Jedrek was jealous that Alesia was with another man, but he could not blame her. He then saw Alesia standing and slowly taking off her clothes. She took off her shirt and bra, exposing her C-cup breasts. She then took off her pants and underwear, showing her womanhood.

Jedrek couldn't take it; he also began to undress.

Alesia lay on the floor, laid her back down, and spread her legs. She did not know what she was doing but knew that she wanted this. She was so excited that she felt her juices dripping down.

Jedrek was fully nude and saw the sight before him. He felt some pre-cum dripping from his erection. He then laid down before her, put the tip of cock on her entrance, and slowly entered her. She was tight and wet. His heart was beating faster every moment. He groaned as he felt her walls clenching onto him. Alesia bit her lower lip. She felt a bit of pain trying to get adjusted to his size.

He noticed this. "I-I'm sorry..."

"Don't be; I need to adjust a bit."

The pain began to subside, and she nodded to him. Jedrek slowly began to move inside her. He let out a groan. His slow movements became faster. He kissed her neck, and his lips trailed to her breasts. Jedrek suckled on each nipple. She moaned as she held his back.

Their moans and groans filled the home as they tried different positions. Their sweat was on one another. Until then, Jedrek groaned as he came inside Alesia, and she let out a loud moan. She felt his cum inside them.

They felt complete.

They were in love.

They were one.

CHAPTER 19

The sun rose, and inside the house, Jedrek felt the sunshine hitting his face. He slowly opened his eyes. He saw Alesia's sleeping form; a smile came across his face. He couldn't deny that yesterday's event was the best thing that ever happened to him. Jedrek felt emotions and sensations that he felt were never possible. It was the first time he had sex. He was taught that sex was nothing more than breeding. Last night, he learned that sex could be intimate. For him, sex was not just a pleasurable activity but a way for two individuals to express their love for one another. Jedrek felt happy that he was given the opportunity. His thoughts were interrupted when he saw Alesia awaking from her slumber. She smiled at him.

"Good morning."

"Good morning to you too. You looked so peaceful that I didn't want to wake you up."

Alesia stretched and then held onto his body, feeling his warmth with her body. "Today is the first day of training."

Jedrek held onto her. "I know; I am not going easy on them. The people we will go against have trained for years and have skills that not even the military has. It's going to be tough."

Alesia sat up from the floor, and Jedrek did the same. "I can't believe that our government can be so cruel. Our leaders have lost the meaning of caring for their people."

"I hate to tell you this, but there are times that greed and distrust are the powerful attributes of human nature. They consume not many, but it can be rare." He then put his arms around Alesia and motioned her face to his.

They kissed. When they separated, both took a shower together and made out even more. Their hands and arms were on one another when they finished showering and ate breakfast.

They got to Alesia's car and drove off in the direction of the place that they were given. Both were a little nervous but knew what had to be done. About thirty-five minutes later, they arrived and saw many cars parked outside the building. The two got out of the car and went inside. When the doors were opened, Fred was with the other soldiers as they were all warming up.

All eyes were on the couple.

"Glad you both made it. I thought you were going to change your minds."

Jedrek chuckled. "Hardly; well, let's get started with training."

....

It has been five days; Jedrek has been training the soldiers while Alesia watched. Jedrek was such a good fighter, as were the other soldiers. However, she was also working with Leo as well. He was considered their eyes since he knew how to use technology. During that time, he created phones and cameras and used drones just in case.

Also, during that time, Jedrek and Alesia spent more time together. Alesia would take him to different places. For Jedrek, he was having the best moments of his life. He would never have imagined that he would feel so much happiness.

It made him realize that no matter what race beings are, love binds many together. At the moment, Jedrek was taking a break with the others, and he sat next to Fred. The two were drinking and talking. "Hey, Jedrek."

"Yeah?"

"Did you know?"

Jedrek raised an eyebrow.

"Since you said your scent is powerful, you can recognize scents. When we first met, you became angry. You knew who my father is."

Jedrek let out a sigh. "Yes, I was shocked that Dr. Antony even had a child."

"I know it is hard to believe, but I remember that he was good once, but his demeanor changed when he began working for the government. He was no longer the man I once knew."

The two young men were silent for a bit. "I asked Leo if Alesia could stay with him for a moment, I don't know why, but I feel that our time is coming. I don't want her to get hurt or killed."

"Good idea; if you want, they can stay at my place when the time comes."

Jedrek's eyes became wide. "You would do that?"

Fred nodded. "Of course, it's the least I can do. My old man made your life a living hell."

"Thank you. Well, we should get on training."

....

Meanwhile, Alesia was at Leo's house, and the two were working on the phones to see if they worked. "You did great work on these, Leo."

"Thanks; my hobby can work out for certain things." Leo eyed Alesia. "Why are you hell-bent on helping that alien? You could have let him leave."

Alesia sighed. "For the last time, I didn't want to leave him alone. How could he survive on his own? He has never seen the outside world. Either way, people could have found out about his identity." She shook her head. "I'm sorry I couldn't return your feelings."

Leo cleared his throat. "I had a sense that you would see me as a friend, but I had to tell you how I felt about you. However, it made me stronger. I am glad that we are still friends."

The young woman smiled. At the same time, she was testing out the phones. She was beginning to feel the need to vomit.

"Hey, are you alright? You don't look so good."

"It's no biggie. I have been feeling nauseated for a while."

Leo raised an eyebrow, and as he was about to speak, there was a knock on the door. He stood and went to open the door. Once he did, many men dressed in combat uniforms entered by force.

Leo and Alesia were in shock. "Alesia, run!" Then one of the soldiers hit Leo with the butt of his gun, making Leo hit him on the wall and land on the floor. He lost consciousness. Alesia screamed and tried to run to another exit of the house. However, she was caught, and The intruders covered her face with a bag.

"Hurry and take her in! We have to make sure that she is not hurt!"

Alesia screamed for help as she was taken into an SUV and driven away.

....

Jedrek felt a painful pang in his heart and put his hand over his chest. He was in the front seat of Fred's jeep, and the soldier took notice. "Hey, are you alright?"

Jedrek didn't answer as he then felt a gut-wrenching feeling in the pit of his stomach. "I-I feel that something's wrong. Is it possible that you can drive a little faster?" Fred raised an eyebrow but drove faster on the highway. To his luck, there were hardly any drivers on the road. Then, Fred went to the road leading to the woods, Alesia and Leo's home. The two knew Alesia was at Leo's house to help with the technology.

As they got closer to Leo's house, Jedrek couldn't help but notice something. There were faint tire tracks. He didn't wait for Fred to park the jeep. Jedrek ran to Leo's house, and when he got to the front porch, he saw that the front door was forcibly broken. He ran inside and saw the interior in disarray.

Fred then ran inside and saw the outcome. Then, the young man saw Leo lying on the floor with blood on his head. "Leo!" He knelt beside his unconscious friend. "Hey, wake up! Leo!"

Jedrek ran throughout the house, calling for Alesia, but she did not answer. He then ran to her place, hoping she would be in her home. The door was unlocked; Jedrek thought it was strange since Alesia always tended to lock the doors. He entered; it was silent, but everything was in place. Jedrek looked around the house, and Alesia was nowhere to be seen.

As he was about to leave the house, he saw a flash drive on the table. He got a hold of it and went back to Leo's house. Leo was put on the couch but was still unconscious. Fred eyed Jedrek. "Can't find her?"

"N-No. I found this on the table in Alesia's house." He handed it to Fred and noticed that Leo's laptop was still on and had slight cracks, but it still worked. He connected the flash drive to the computer. Then a video popped up.

"Hello, my little half-breed. It has been a while since you have escaped."

It was Dr. Antony, sitting on a comfortable chair.

Jedrek growled in rage. Fred was filled with shock to see his father.

"You have caused us so much trouble, and I miss your presence. We have lost resources, and the government is going a little berserk. However, I am not too worried. I am sure you enjoyed the bit of freedom that I allowed you to have. Especially with that woman that took you in."

Jedrek growled; his breathing was becoming rapid.

"However, freedom comes at a price. Now I must ask you to come back. Yet, I knew you would not come back lightly since you have been training others and my son."

Antony laughed.

Fred shook his head. "He knows about us."

"We took your little mate, and she will be in the facility. If you want her back, you know what you must do."

Antony sighed.

"As for you, Fred. If you interfere, I will not be afraid to harm you. This is your first and only warning. Half-breed, you have three days to think about it, or the woman will get it. Enjoy your last bits of freedom.

" He laughed.

"Yet, I know you will return to me. I look forward to seeing you again."

The video turned off.

Jedrek punched a hole in the wall. "He has her! Alesia was taken!" He had never felt so hopeless.

CHAPTER 20

er body felt weak, and she couldn't move properly. "Leo! Jedrek!"

"My, my, you're awake," said a masculine voice.

Dr. Antony entered with both hands in his coat pockets on the other side of the room.

"Wh-Who...?"

"Yes, you and I never met, but my colleagues and I have kept an eye on you. My name is Dr. Antony. You must be Alesia, the mate that my half-breed has chosen."

Alesia got a hold of the bedsheets, pulled herself on them, and sat down. She couldn't run or fight. "So you are the one that held Jedrek in this place?"

Dr. Antony chuckled. "Jedrek, is that the name you have given him?" He let out a laugh. "I never heard such a name. However, to answer your question, he has been kept here for a good cause."

"You're using him for selfish needs and wants, just like this government! You only hurt him! You killed his parents and forced them into a life they never asked for!"

"Ha! Ha! If I remember correctly, Yesele was seen as an eyesore of society since she lived in foster care. Even when she got out of foster care, she wouldn't have made it in the real world. As for the alien, he was the only of his kind that we know of. We did them both a favor."

Alesia glared at him. "You and everyone here have no heart! So you took me to make Jedrek come here."

The man chuckled. "Of course, it is quite obvious. However, there is another reason. We also see you as an important asset we can't lose yet."

This confused the young woman. "What are you talking about?" Then she began to feel pain in her stomach and felt nauseated. "What did you do to me!?"

"I guess you don't know. I didn't do anything to you, my dear. It was you, and the half-breed did with each other. As I said before, you are now important to us for more specific reasons. Since you are to stay here until the half-breed arrives, we will care for you. I know the half-breed will not arrive in a while since he is training those soldiers." Dr. Antony left the room.

Alesia was filled with confusion about what he told her. Her nausea came again as well as the pain. She threw up. That was when the realization came to her. "Oh my god."

She put her hand over her womb.

....

Dr. Antony arrived in Dr. Logan's office. "What is the status of her condition?" asked Logan.

"She is going well, for now. However, she has been giving the guards a hard time. Yet, she knows she has no choice but to eat and drink." Dr. Logan stopped looking at the paperwork and looked concerned.

Antony knew what was bothering Logan; he rolled his eyes. "You are still thinking about the half-breed?"

"Well, yes. It's the final day when he has to decide to come back. Do you think he decided to abandon his mate?"

"The half-breed has grown close with her. I am thinking that they are training even more." Dr. Antony chuckled. "I expected as much; I look forward to it."

Dr. Logan raised his eyebrows. "The government is getting even more restless; we are very close to losing our funding. It will be the end of our work!"

"You worry too much. The government can have all its threats. I am getting tired of working for those foolish old men. They can cut the funding if they wish. They can never get the information and power that we hold. They know this, which is why they won't even dare. Power is what drives them."

Logan massaged the top of his head. "Let's hope so."

Chapter 21

The soldiers were well-equipped and had tiny earphones where they could hear and communicate with one another. They also watched with maps and locators. Leo was at his home as he was the group's eyes and ears. He built technology that would help them on their mission.

Jedrek at first wanted to go immediately to rescue Alesia, but Fred urged and convinced him that it was not a good idea. Jedrek was the only one who knew more of the facility while the other did not. Fred wanted Jedrek to help him as a spy and study the facility to take videos and pictures.

Fred used them to train the others on how they would enter. They found a secret compartment that was the long way to get inside the main facility. There were a few guards that were on guard of the secret passage.

Fred and another male soldier carefully got out of their hiding spot and went to the two guards. "Break," said Fred.

"We haven't seen you here before," said one of the guards.

"Barely hired. Our superiors wanted us to guard here for a start."

The two guards were suspicious. "Our superiors would have informed us of new hires."

Fred and the other soldier took out their ids and showed them to the guards. The guards eyed them carefully. One of them was about to get the radio. "We are going to contact our superiors to make sure." Suddenly, Fred and his partner kicked them, making them lose balance, and they both got a hold of their head, and a snap was heard. The bodies of guards were then dragged to some bushes. The others went to the two and got the secret passage open, and one by one, they all entered.

They were now in the facility. Jedrek's eye color changed. "Follow me; it's time to move."

Their mission began.

....

Once inside the secret passage of the facility, the group were together and followed Jedrek, who led them to different paths. To their surprise, the directions were like a maze, and everything looked similar. However, Jedrek could see through the walls with his vision. Jedrek was happy to recognize most of the facility since he was taken to many parts of it when he was imprisoned.

Suddenly, Fred commanded everyone to stop. Jedrek also stopped but was confused why he would stop abruptly.

"Knowing my pops, he is very prepared for many situations. He will not let just anyone break into the facility. I know he would have traps."

"That's true. Even though the facility is heavily guarded, Dr. Logan and Antony will not be so careless to think of the worst-case scenario. What are you thinking?"

Fred looked at his men. "We will need to split up, but Jedrek and I will go together and find Alesia. I know they are keeping an eye on her." He then motioned everyone to gather together and told everyone the plan.

"Are you sure about this? It might be risky. What happens if they don't believe it?" asked one of the soldiers.

"We have no other options. We have to do anything to get Alesia and survive."

Jedrek let out a sigh. "Alright, I'll trust your judgment."

Fred nodded and ordered his group to scatter, leaving the two men alone. Jedrek then led Fred to different parts of the facility, climbing up a vent to avoid being seen by guards. To their luck, the vent was not loud to make noises. With Jedrek's eyesight, he could see many prison rooms.

They were getting closer and closer and got on top of the prison rooms, and Jedrek looked everywhere; there was no sign of Alesia. However, as they went further, he saw an image of her in the last room, sitting on the bed. "I found her!"

Fred nodded and informed the others, including Leo. The two were on top of the prison room. Jedrek used his nails to make a hole. He took the piece out and put it to the side when it was complete.

Alesia was lost in thought inside the prison room as she looked at the empty walls. However, she heard something up in the ceiling. Then there was a large hole. Her eyes became wide open as Jedrek stood in front of her.

The two looked at one another as if trying to ensure they looked at actual people. Alesia stood and went to hug him. Jedrek felt her body on his. Their warmth was on the other. However, Jedrek felt something on his stomach when the two separated. Jedrek looked down, and his eyes became wide open. "Y-You are..."

Alesia put a hand over her belly. "Yes, they kept me here until the baby is born."

Jedrek was overwhelmed by the shock that he did not realize that tears were dripping from his eyes. Alesia is pregnant with their child. They were going to be parents, and now he was determined to get Alesia out of here.

"What a moment," said a masculine voice.

Jedrek flinched, as did Alesia. When they turned, they saw Dr. Antony, Dr. Logan, and their men. They have been caught.

Jedrek felt his body rage as he saw the two men who brought him so much suffering and tormented him all his life. He knew that they never changed. However, he didn't think about his survival anymore, but it was more for Alesia and their unborn child. He stood before her, keeping her close to him.

Dr.Antony and Dr. Logan chuckled. "Well, we are delighted that you came back to us. We were worried sick if you went to the wrong hands," said Dr. Logan.

"Still cruel as ever."

"My, my. After all, we have done for you. I don't know why you would even escape from us. We have fed, trained, and given you a roof over your head. What more did you want?" asked Dr. Antony.

Jedrek growled. "Freedom. Something that you took away from my parents and me. You only wanted me for your gain."

Dr. Antony stepped forward. "You would have been given a purpose. You would have had power beyond your imagination. You could have been the best killer alive and would have brought so much from our research from your alien heritage."

"Bullshit! You tortured me as if I was nothing. You made my mother and father as breeding tools for your sick gain. They wanted me to have a better life than this, so I left."

"And now you came back, for your precious mate." Dr.Antony clapped his hands. "You have done much of the work for us. We would have chosen a female mate, but you chose one yourself. She will provide us with more answers now that she is pregnant."

Jedrek growled as his eyes glowed. The guards pointed their machine guns toward the couple. Jedrek held Alesia close to him. Alesia felt scared and put her hands over her womb. She was more afraid for their unborn child's life.

"Don't worry; we will not kill both of you. You two are critical to us, especially you, dear sweet Alesia. You carry another half-breed in you, which can be very valuable to our research, to see how long the alien lineage lasts and how its powers get affected."

"Like hell, I would let you monsters get a hold of our baby! Don't any of you have a heart!? You have a family!"

Dr. Antony looked amused. "Sacrifices must be made for the greater good. My research can make a difference in this world. I know my family would understand this." Dr. Antony looked behind him and smiled. "Right, son?"

Alesia flinched, as did Jedrek. "What?"

The couple heard footsteps and the guards made their way.

"No, it can't be! Fred, what?"

Chapter 22

F red stepped forward, expressionless. His eyes seemed dead to the world. Jedrek snarled as his fangs grew bigger. "I should have known! That's why you decided to take control of the group! Leo! Did he...!?"

Fred could hear Leo at the other end of his earphone, screaming. He turned it off and shrugged. "He's an idiot. It was easy to fool him. I only took an interest in him for his gadgets and ensured he didn't dig deep in things he shouldn't have."

Alesia felt angry tears forming in her eyes. "How long have you-!?"

"He's my pops. I've been in contact with him once in a while."

"Those soldiers of yours they...?" asked Jedrek.

"They were easy to bribe."

Dr. Antony patted his son's shoulder. "He is like me every day. My son informed me of everything that had been going on. That's how we got your hiding spot and everything happening. He brought you to us."

"Well, pops, I'll wait for you in the office." Fred walked out. Jedrek screamed, and the guards got a hold of him. Jedrek fought and tried to get to Alesia, but she pulled away from him. The two let out their hands, trying to reach each other, but they were dragged away.

"Oh, don't worry, you two will see each other again. However, we have something in store for you, our little half-breed. Later on, we will test you out against one of our subjects that you would be interested in. As for you, my dear will keep watch. We do want you to be his motivation. Take him away and give him the necessary food and drinks. He will need all his strength on what will happen next," said Dr. Logan.

Alesia was pushed back, and the door closed. She banged on the door. From afar, she could hear Jedrek screaming for her.

....

Jedrek was chained to the wall; he could not move. He was locked in a white room that was only brick and had no window. He didn't care about his well-being but more for Alesia's. Jedrek knew it wouldn't be easy, but he did not expect Alesia to be pregnant with his child. He was afraid for them both and knew that Dr. Antony and Logan would never let her leave and him either.

"Hey, Jedrek! Can you hear me?"

said a voice.

Jedrek almost forgot that he still had the earpiece and was still connected to Leo. "Mmmhmm. Yeah, but I can't talk too loudly, or they will be suspicious."

"I heard everything that was happening. Are you sure the plan is going to work?"

Jedrek chuckled. "I knew this would happen, and some of us would not make out of here alive."

It was silent on the other end.

"I also heard about Alesia. Is it true that she's...?"

"Yeah." Jedrek was silent for a bit. "Hey Leo, could I ask you for a favor? I know we haven't known each other long, but what I am about to ask you is the favor of a lifetime."

"Yeah...sure..."

Jedrek whispered something to Leo, and when he was done, Leo was silent.

"What are you trying to say?"

"You know, Leo. Please."

"What you told me is crazy. It's as if...!"

"Leo. Please."

Leo let out a long sigh.

"Okay, I promise."

Suddenly, the door opened; six guards entered. They all had weapons. The guards unchained him from the wall and got a hold of him. However, Jedrek did not fight, as he was forced to walk to wherever they were taking him.

Flashbacks came to him when he was a child as he was forced through the corridors. He was being taken to an arena, where he was forced to fight with other soldiers. He knew Dr. Antony and Logan were cruel and sadistic and planning something vile, but he did not know what.

After what seemed like forever, he finally made it to the arena. The arena was dark, but the lights came on, and there were guards. Fred and his men were standing in the upper parts of the stadium. The two scientists stood in the center and walked toward him.

"We hope you relaxed enough because today will be a glorious day."

"What's so glorious about it? Whenever you have something glorious, you think of something sick."

"Quite rude. You must have inherited it from your human mother. No matter, after all, we have done for you, I think it's time you show us how strong you are, especially since you have a human side. You are going to fight," said Dr. Antony.

Jedrek glared at the men. "If I refuse?"

Dr. Antony snapped his fingers, and then a part of the wall opened. Alicia was seen tied to a pole. "Then she and your child will be harmed. I have no qualms about killing your mate; the unborn can easily be ripped from her."

Alesia was crying while Fred and the others looked at her and Jedrek.

Jedrek bit his lower lip. "Okay, I'll fight."

"Good boy. Now, let's bring your opponent."

Then another part of the wall opened; five other scientists entered with a sizeable container-like pod and put it in front of them. One of the scientists put in a code, and the pod opened.

Dr. Antony smiled. "Come along and walk forward."

The figure walked out of the pod. Jedrek's eyes were wide open in horror, as were his lips. Fred and his men were also in shock.

"We have always wanted to see this go and about. This is who you will fight. Say hello to your father."

CHAPTER 23

Jedrek and everyone in the arena were in shock. Jedrek's father walked out of the pod and stopped mid-way. "H-How ca-can this be!? I-I thought he was...."

"Killed? I know; it was what we had to tell you. He was almost about to die, but luckily we were there in time; we made a few adjustments. We got control of his brain, which took years to perfect, but eventually, he is under our control and will do what we ask of it." Antony smiled. "Genius, if I say so myself."

Alesia was horrified and struggled. "You people are monsters! Devils! How could you do this!? Trying to force father and son to fight!?"

"Oh, my dear, it's something you will never understand. It is for the greater good of science and advancement. Don't you realize the wonders we are doing? True, it can be seen as cruel, but bad things happened to make good things occur throughout history. People need to be sacrificed for the greater good of many."

"Bullshit! You all are working for a government that doesn't give a shit for their people!"

Antony laughed and merely shrugged his shoulders. "Believe what you want, my dear. Either way, we will get what we want. You will pay for the consequences if your little half-breed lover doesn't do what we say."

Jedrek felt his body shake as he looked at his father, who had never seen him before. "What about my mother? Is she. ..?"

"Dead, I'm afraid. You killed your mother when you were born. I will admit, she died for the greater good."

Jedrek felt rage and went towards him, but the guards stopped him.

"Now, now, there's no need to get angry. You know what you have to do. We need to see once and for all who is stronger, a half-breed or full-bred alien. Decide."

Jedrek looked at Alesia and then at his father. Everything was going downhill. He now met his father, but his father may not know or recognize him as he controlled. Alesia is pregnant with their child, and he wants nothing more than their safety. He calmed himself as his eyes were on his motionless father.

"Excellent, now you two shall begin." Antony, Logan, and the guards stepped out of the way, and now it was Jedrek and his father. His father growled, and Jedrek's eyes changed as he also growled.

"I'm so sorry." Then, Jedrek used his speed to punch his father; the alien dodged and punched Jedrek on his stomach. Jedrek groaned in pain, but he held his stance. Suddenly, the alien used his super-speed and was behind Jedrek and tried to scratch him, but he barely moved away from him.

The two ran towards one another and collided, holding the other's hands. Their eyes were on another.

The true fight has begun.

Alesia was horrified at the sight of her. Jedrek was forced to fight his father, who he thought was killed when he was born. It also made her feel the rage that such men would be so cruel to make both of them fight one another for their gain. She couldn't fathom thinking that one or both of them might die. Alesia didn't want Jedrek to get killed, but she did not want his father to die either.

Both suffered in the hands of man.

Jedrek growled and went towards his father with super speed, and his father did the same. They clashed. They got a hold of one another; Jedrek did a kick on his father's face, but it seemed to have no effect. His father didn't even flinch. Before the alien was about to strike, Jedrek knew this; he immediately moved away.

He was taking deep breaths. He never fought like this. He only fought and killed other humans, who he thought were easier to kill, but fighting his father, a pureblood alien, was much more complex than he could admit. Worse, his father was being controlled to fight for the humans, making him and his mother suffer. His eyes then trailed to Alesia, who was filled with fear.

Jedrek didn't want Alesia and their child to have the same fate as him and his mother. He wanted his mate and unborn child to live a free and happy life without continuing the cycle. He noticed his father hissing at him.

"I can't win against him like this,"

he told himself. He realized that he could no longer fight in his human form. Jedrek began to undress until he was fully nude.

Many were confused, but the scientists smirked. "It is coming," said Dr. Logan. Suddenly, everyone watched as Jedrek's body began to crack and change into a different form. His skin became a different color; he became taller, and his features became monstrous. Jedrek was no longer in his human form but his alien form.

He let out a loud screech, and his father did the same thing. The two then ran towards one another and collided again. An aftershock was felt throughout the stadium as their collisions were powerful. The two would punch one another, but Jedrek did not feel the same pain as he used to in his human form. He thought that he could match his father in his alien form.

The two would use their super-speed to attack or dodge.

The fight filled the scientists with amazement as they enjoyed watching the scenery.

Jedrek then made a large scratch on his father's waist, and a green liquid would drip. The half-breed realized what he had done. He then realized that he would kill his father. The thought of that made him feel terrified. He finally met his father, and now that he was before him and fighting to the death, it just made him feel fear.

A son to kill his father, a father to kill his son. A tear dripped from one of his eyes and leaked to the floor.

His father stood there motionless, trying to comprehend what Jedrek was doing.

Everyone watched as the father and son stood still, looking at one another. Alesia noticed that Jedrek's father was still when he saw Jedrek shed a tear. It made her wonder if his father could break free of mind control. She wanted to yell out, but if she did, then the scientist would have a trick up their sleeves.

Jedrek saw his father standing still when he shed a tear. It surprised him. Maybe, just maybe, he could free him after all. He did have a chance to be on his level in his alien form, but the more he stayed in his alien form, the less chance his father would be freed from the brain control. That was when he decided to change back to his human form. He was nude but put on his clothing.

The scientists and the onlookers were confused.

"What is he doing? Is he mad?" asked Dr. Logan.

Dr. Antony didn't respond. His hands were crossed. He had to admit that he was curious, but at the same time, it made him think about whether or not Jedrek had a plan. "This will be interesting," he told himself.

Jedrek then lifted his arms. "I am your son. I was born here. You were also taken from your homeland and brought here against your will. You were used and experimented on by the scientists by this facility."

Fred and the others kept on looking. He bit his lip but did not say a word. He looked at his father and noticed his serious expression.

"They wanted you to procreate, to see how your offspring would turn out. They lied and brought my human mother, Yesele, to this facility. She was told and promised she would have a good life, but it was far from the truth. She was scared and was to be your mate for breeding. She was afraid of you, but when she saw how much you suffered, she realized that you two were not so different from one another."

Dr. Antony saw how the alien did not move as it stood there and listened. He made sure that the alien was under his control. Nothing could break it. "Alien! Attack him."

The alien felt a jolt within his mind and body. He roared and went towards Jedrek. Jedrek was punched in the stomach, making him hit the wall.

"Jedrek!" screamed Alesia.

Jedrek coughed. He lay on the ground. "When you and my mother made love, my mother wanted you both to escape from here to have freedom since she was pregnant with me. You both wanted a better life for me." He slowly stood on his own two feet. "However, you two were caught, and my mother died giving birth to me. I thought you were killed when you ran for her. To be close to her. Your mate, your love that knew your suffering. She died because of them!" he pointed to the scientists.

"Attack him! Destroy him, alien!" commanded Dr. Logan.

To everyone's surprise, the alien did not move. His entire body shook. "Attack him now!" The alien lost control and went towards his son; Jedrek did not move away. His father grabbed him by the neck and forced him to the wall. His father was squeezing his neck.

Jedrek got to hold his father's hand. "I went through the same things you did. I was experimented on, but I never lost hope. I escaped, felt freedom for the first time, and met Alesia, who gave me a name that brought me happiness, even for a short time." He smiled as he felt tears forming and dripping down from his eyes. "Father, my name is Jedrek. I am your son. Please, father." He was feeling lightheaded as his father's grip tightened.

His tears dripped on his father's hand. The alien watched and listened to what Jedrek said. He felt the tears on his hand.

He growled and looked at Jedrek closely. Suddenly, the alien felt a sharp pain in his mind.

"What is going on!?" asked Dr. Logan.

Dr. Antony looked at his iPad. "What in the?" He saw that the mind control chip was malfunctioning. His eyes widened. "Guards, seize the alien and the half-breed immediately!" The guards flinched at the sudden command but went to follow their orders. Jedrek was catching his breath and noticed the guards coming toward them.

The guards caught up to him and got a hold of him, Jedrek struggled and tried using his strength, but he was shocked by the tasers. As for his father, he howled in pain as he held onto his head.

Fred and the other looked on. "This is about enough." He took out his handgun and shot the iPad from his father's hands. "I had enough with this bullshit. You never changed pops."

Dr. Antony shook his head. "You were playing around. I had a hunch, but I had a little sense a hope you would change the error of your ways. I guess that was the biggest mistake." He snapped his fingers, and more guards entered the arena. "Kill him and the others, but take the girl."

Fred and the other got their weapons and opened fire.

Meanwhile, the alien saw Jedrek being tased and screaming in pain. Then, he felt a jolt in his brain. He squealed and scratched the guards away from him and ran towards Jedrek. He punched the guards away from him.

Jedrek was about to fall to the floor, but his father held him.

Jedrek looked up and saw that his father was looking at him. The two were face to face. Then, the alien slowly put his hand on Jedrek's head and softly stroked his hair. Jedrek felt more tears forming and smiled.

"You remember."

The full-breed alien finally got out of the brain control and remembered everything. Yesele, her death, and the cries of their child. However, he was not fully able to see his newborn child.

The alien looked down, slowly put his hand over his hair, and patted him. He realized that the male looked like his deceased mate, Yesele. He was her spitting image but felt another aura within him and realized that Jedrek inherited his alien genes. It was his son. He let out a slight soft growl.

Even though he could not speak the human tongue, the alien felt happy that his son survived and was before him.

"Father, we don't have time. My mate, Alesia, is held captive, and we must save her. She is also pregnant with our child." Jedrek looked at Alesia, who was crying with joy. All of a sudden, the wall opened, forcing her inside.

Alesia screamed while Jedrek tried to get to her, but it was too late, and he couldn't get her on time. Fred saw this and glared at his father, who merely smirked. "I sensed that you were lying, so I had to take extra precautions. The guards then got in front of him and Dr. Logan and motioned them to run, which they did so. The guards opened fire, but Fred and the others got out of harm's way.

They got their weapons and also returned fire.

The whole scene looked like war.

Chapter 24

Then, everyone in the arena heard a loud alarm throughout the facility; Jedrek knew there would be reinforcements. He went to his father. "We have to go after them. They have Alesia; I can't let them hurt her.

The alien understood. He let out a roar as the guards aimed their guns toward him and Jedrek. The alien used his super-speed and sliced their necks. Blood spurted out.

Jedrek saw this and went to Fred and the others to help. He also used his speed to kill the guards. Fred and the others came out from their hiding places. "Seems you didn't fool your father as we thought."

"Guess not," said Fred as he let out a sigh.

"My father and I will give chase to them. I need you and the others to do something that will end this place. Leo will give you all the specifics."

"You are going alone?" asked Fred.

"My father will join me. Now please hurry."

Fred and his friends eyed one another but nodded and went on their way. The alien climbed up and was by his son's side. "We need to hurry and get to those bastards. I have to save my mate." Father and son gave chase to the two men that had made them miserable.

Dr. Logan and Dr. Antony were walking on a hidden path. Dr. Logan would look behind him now and then. "We have to get out of here as soon as we can! We must wait for the signal when the enemy has been exterminated!"

Antony did not say a word or even look at Dr. Logan; he walked ahead. Dr. Logan noticed that Antony got out of the secret pathway and into another room. Inside, there were many hazardous liquids in containers. There were also weapons, armor, and much more. Logan followed, feeling confused in the process. "What in blazes are you doing!? We have to escape! They also have to get to the girl and take her to the other facility since she holds our other test subject."

"I have come too far."

Dr. Logan stilled. "What?"

Antony then went to a compartment and took out a veil with green liquid. He then held the injection and filled it with the liquid. "I have come so far. I am not going to let those fools ruin everything. We tested those aliens for too long; I thought they had the answer, but they showed me that I was wrong."

"What are you talking about!? We don't have time for this! We have to leave and take the girl with us! Those things will be after us."

Dr. Antony gave out the most giant and evil smirk he could muster as he held the injection filled with the liquid. "That is what I want them to do. Let them come here. I will finally test my last experiment and see once and for all who is the strongest."

Logan's eyes widened. "Wait, don't tell that it is..."

"Yes, I have taken some of the DNA of the pureblood alien. I have fixed it so it wouldn't be lethal to whoever fills it with their own. I will inject its DNA into mine to see who is superior."

"You are insane! It hasn't been tested yet! It could kill you!"

Antony took off his lab coat and lifted the sleeves, exposing his entire arm. "I am willing to take the risk." Then, he injected the needle into his vein, putting the liquid within him."

....

Jedrek and his father ran through the halls, using their vision to try to find the scientists. They went by many of the guards, but the father and son duo took them down. Then, the alien noticed something in one of the rooms and communicated with Jedrek. Jedrek followed his father, and the two went towards the room. The door was opened; the duo went inside.

The duo stopped in their tracks and became shocked. They saw Dr. Logan lying by a wall filled with horror. Then, Antony screamed in pain as his bones cracked loudly and painfully. His skin opened, and his muscles were visible, but then he grew bigger and longer, and his skin turned into scales. His hands and feet became longer and had claws. His face became deformed at first but then developed into a long length. Antony's hair fell off; his eyes had thin slints and were black red. He had eight tentacles on his back. He was taller and bigger than the alien and Jedrek's alien form.

"What in the hell!?"

Antony was no longer human. To Jedrek, he didn't even look like an alien.

Antony was now a monster.

All watched in horror at Antony's new form. He was bigger than Jedrek and his father.

"What have you become?"

Jedrek asked in a faint whisper.

Antony's monster form growled, but then a huge smirk was apparent. "What am I?" he asked in a low and dangerous tone. "I am what I have researched and created. I am the future. I am power." He eyed father and son. "All those years, I have tested your DNA, trying to make clones and weapons, but nothing worked. However, I decided to test something that might have been considered insane and dangerous. Transmutation of alien DNA with a human's. Never before has this been tested, until now."

Jedrek felt sweat forming behind his neck. "You are insane. You always were."

"I consider myself a genius, a hope for humans alike. Don't you realize that I can achieve greatness!? Yet, you had to ruin it. Well, it doesn't matter anymore. You two are no longer needed. Now that your little girlfriend is pregnant with your child, I will use that child to strengthen my power and research. No one will be getting in my way."

Jedrek growled. "Where's Alesia!?"

"Don't worry, she is safe, for now. I have no intention of killing her since she carries the future. You should be more worried about yourselves. Especially since you all are going to die."

Logan was in pure shock. He never knew that Antony experimented with such things. The two would usually work together, but this made him realize how ambitious and insane Antony was. "Antony! You need to change back to your old form! You haven't tested this experiment to its full extent! There could be drastic consequences."

Logan was ignored, and he ran towards him, but suddenly, Antony slashed him in half. Blood, guts, and body parts were scattered. Jedrek and his father were shocked but kept their calm composure. "He was always annoying but useful for my success."

"You always cared about yourself."

"Why, of course, it is the duty of the weak to serve the strong until they are rendered useless."

Jedrek shook his head. "You are such a pitiful human. You lived a sad life, not caring for anyone but yourself. You don't even love your son. You made me, my father, and my mother suffer, but we must thank you."

Antony growled.

"You gave us the motivation to live, love, and keep living. Meanwhile, you never had anything, to begin with."

Without warning, Antony grew tentacles out from his back and whipped Jedrek and his father in opposite directions, making them hit the wall so hard that it made large cracks. Jedrek felt pain in his body and changed into his alien form. He knew that his human form was no match for Antony's monster form.

His father got on his feet and growled, as did Jedrek. Father and son let out roars as a declaration of battle. The two ran towards Antony. Antony used his tentacles to get a hold of them, but the father and son duo dodged and punched him in the gut, making him hit the wall this time.

Antony and the two aliens eyed one another. They all knew their lifetime's absolute and final fight had begun, and the end was coming.

Father and son were in their alien forms and charged at Dr. Antony's monstrous form. Antony did not charge. Instead, he used his tentacles to get a hold of the duo, but the two would dodge from place to place. The two were quick, but it did not deter Antony. He also used his super-speed and got behind on both of them.

Jedrek and his father were shocked since they couldn't see Antony. Antony punched both, and it made them both hit the wall. Cracks were caused on the wall. The duo hissed at Antony. Suddenly, Antony was in front of them and got a hold of their necks. Jedrek stabbed Antony in the arm; some blood splurted out. Antony seemed unfazed. "Ha! Ha! You both think that will be enough. Fools!"

Antony then used two tentacles to stab Jedrek, but the half-breed got a hold of them; Jedrek couldn't believe how strong Antony was, but he refused to give in.

The pureblood hissed louder and began to move faster and harder, he also got his sharp nails and then punctured Antony's other arm, but this time, he cut off the arm, making Antony lose his grip. The pureblood then cut off the other arm, freeing Jedrek. Jedrek let go of the tentacles, and the two went off to their distance.

Both of them knew it would not be easy and didn't know if they were even going to live in this fight.

....

Meanwhile, Fred and the others were trying to find Alesia. On the other end, Leo used the signals he created to try to find her. Leo could hear the gunfire from Fred's part. He would never have imagined that he and the others would be in this situation. Fred and Jedrek did plan the betrayal well. He fell for it, but now he was concerned for Alesia's safety. He was trying the very best he could find any trace of her.

"Hey Leo, any trace!?" asked Fred.

"I'm trying! I-! Hold on!

" He saw figures moving around in a specific room.

"Hey, I see a struggle in a garage-like room, and there seems to be a struggle. Turn to your left, and it will be a large door in your front!"

"Got it! Fred and the others ran to where Leo commanded them to go. They got to the door where Leo said, and it was opened. Fred and his men saw Alesia being dragged forcibly into a large jeep. She was struggling to get out of their grip. Fred gave his men hand signals and knew what they meant. They all spread out while Fred remained in the middle and began to shoot. He shot and killed one of the soldiers who held onto Alesia.

The soldiers were shocked; many began to shoot. Fred moved out of the way in time. Alesia was able to get out of the other soldiers' grip and ran to another side of the room to make sure not to be hit. Bullets were everywhere, and a few missed Alesia by sheer luck. She then crawled over a pile of wooden boxes that would give her more protection.

One of the soldiers saw her and was about to go to her, but he was shot down by one of Fred's army buddies. Alesia noticed the soldier who saved her, motioning her to get closer to them. That was what she did, but she was sure not to get in the way.

Fred saw her and ran to her while shooting at the enemy. He finally got to her and ran to get her to safety. However, he got shot in his left arm. He yelped in pain. "Fred!" Alesia screamed.

Fred got a hold of the grenade, and everyone in his team ran out of the garage. Fred threw the grenade while closing the door. There was a loud bang at the other end, and everything went silent. Fred groaned as he felt the bullet on his arm. One of his buddies went to take the shot out and stop the bleeding.

Alesia was horrified.

"Don't worry, Alesia. I'll be okay. You were our top priority."

"At least you all are alive! Where's Jedrek!?"

"He is after my father and his partner. He told me to get you out of here."

"I won't leave him behind!"

Fred was about to respond, but Alesia began to run. Fred and the others called out to her, and they had no choice but to run after her.

....

Jedrek and his father were pinned to the wall by Antony's tentacles on his back. Jedrek broke free by cutting them. He noticed that his father was wounded and was getting weaker.

He knew that brain control took a considerable toll on his entire body.

Yet, things never go as they should. Jedrek heard an explosion from afar, and these thoughts trailed to Alesia. He was concerned about her but knew that she was in good hands. "Something's off," he told himself. He couldn't help but notice that Antony's moves were getting slower and that Antony was breathing faster and deeper, even though he was trying to hide it.

Jedrek used his super-speed and went to his father, cutting him free from Antony's grasp and taking them far from him. His father was breathing heavily. He then eyed Antony's monster form. "You're getting slower. I found it strange that you were very boastful and filled with energy initially, but now I'm noticing that your moves were not as they were a moment ago. I then remembered that Logan said your experiment hadn't been thoroughly tested, which means there are still risks.

Antony growled and used his speed to attack the duo, but they dodged it easily.

"I thought so. You're getting weaker and slower. The alien blood you took from us has taken its toll on your own human body. You probably didn't have much time to study it."

"Bah! Nonsense! I have studied it for years! My brilliance has never once failed me!"

Jedrek shook his head. "True, you have studied us for many years, but you forgot that you haven't studied my father's true origins. True, you found him elsewhere, but there is a possibility that his origins are from elsewhere. One's environment can greatly affect their physical and emotional development. My father was hiding more secrets than you could comprehend. Your pride and ignorance got the best of you. The blood you took will surely kill you."

Antony felt anger boil within him. He refused to admit that he was wrong. He thought that he did everything perfectly and promptly. "Ha! You're nothing more than a half-breed! I realize that you all are no longer needed! I have your woman and her unborn child! I will use them to-!" He didn't finish as a massive sensation of pain filled him.

The pain was so severe that it made him lose his balance. "What's going on!?" he asked himself. He felt his body acting strangely. It was as if he was losing control of it.

"I told you. The blood reacts to your body; your human side cannot control and withstand it. It's taking its effect."

Antony shook his head and wanted to attack, but suddenly, his arm grew more prominent. It became bigger and bigger; it was too painful. Then more tentacles formed all over his body. He screamed. "What's going on! What's happening to me!?"

Jedrek and his father watched Antony lose control of his body and become deformed. One of his arms exploded. "We need to leave as soon as possible, father. He is not going to last that long."

"Jedrek!"

The half-breed stilled for a moment and then turned. He saw Alesia standing by the exit. He felt his heart skip a beat. He smiled and felt tears form in his eyes. "Alesia." He thought it was a dream, but she ran to him and hugged him. "It's not a dream; you're here." He hugged her back.

Fred then came afterward, trying to regain his breath. "At least you both are okay!"

The alien watched as his son and his mate embraced. He then remembered Yesele, his human mate. He let out a soft growl favoring the moment.

Antony was becoming bigger and bigger, and he knew he was about to explode. He couldn't believe that he had failed.

All his work and research were for not. He was going to die by his hand. He then saw Alesia and the others together. He refused to submit! He would die but refused to die without having his enemies standing. "If I die, I will take you all with me!" With the last strength, he used a tentacle headed to Jedrek and Alesia.

Fred saw this. "Jedrek, Alesia, look out!"

Jedrek turned and saw the tentacle getting closer, and then...*SPLAT*

Epilogue

"Dad!" yelled Jedrek as he went to his father, who was gasping. The alien's blood slowly poured to the floor, and Jedrek put his hand over his father's wound. "Fred, anyone! Please!"

Fred immediately knelt beside the alien and looked at the damage. Fred knew his father had punctured the alien's heart by looking at it. He was unable to do anything.

Jedrek noticed the look on Fred's face and got a hold of his shirt. "Fred!"

"I'm sorry..."

Jedrek eyed the others, and they all held a defeated look on their faces. He shook his head as he looked at his father. Alesia knelt beside Jedrek, hugging him. The pureblood alien felt his blood dripping; he knew he would die. The alien looked at his son and saw a few tears forming. He wiped them off his son's eyes. Jedrek looked at his father.

"Father..."

The alien looked at his son and Alesia. Slowly and gently, the alien grabbed Alesia and Jedrek's hands and put them together. It was as if he was telling them to go and be happy.

Alesia couldn't hold back her tears as she held onto Jedrek's hand tightly; he did the same. As for the alien, he felt his breathing weaker and lost strength. However, he then saw the image of Yesele before him. She was smiling at him. Yesele wore a strapless white dress; her hair had many small yellow flowers. Yesele knelt beside him and touched his face and then gave him a peck on his head.

She then stood up and motioned out her right hand.

"It's time to go home."

The alien got a hold of her hand and stood before her. Both looked at one another. The alien felt at peace and happy to be with his mate. He hugged her; Yesele did the same, and their bodies dissipated.

Jedrek cried as he put his forehead on his father's forehead. Alesia hugged Jedrek. The alien had died. Then, the building was shaking, and more alarms went out. Fred stood up.

"Jedrek, I'm sorry, but we need to go."

Jedrek looked at his father's dead body and slowly stood up, as did Alesia. "Let's go. This place will explode; there will be reinforcements coming." Jedrek held onto Alesia; he led the others to get out of the facility.

As the ground shook, everyone ran as fast as their legs could carry them. As they ran, they dodged many objects and crumbled from the ceiling and walls of the facility. For Jedrek, so many thoughts were going through his head, but the most important thing was Alesia's safety. While running, everyone noticed Alesia was getting exhausted, especially since she was pregnant.

Jedrek got a hold of her bridal style as they all ran. Fred felt pain where he was shot but knew he had to go through. There were times when they ran by other guards and soldiers that tried to shoot them, but Fred and his other comrades would shoot them down. The alarm became louder and louder.

"We don't have time left!" yelled Jedrek.

"Guys, I found an exit close to where you guys are! I will instruct you all!" yelled Leo at the other end of the line.

Everyone listened as Leo instructed them to go through many passageways. They all saw an exit, and they were relieved as they ran. Moments later, they made it outside the facility but kept running.

Then-

BAM!

An explosion was heard; many parts of the facility exploded. The nearby city also heard the explosion, and many saw it afar. Many people called the police.

As for Jedrek and the others, many were on the ground; some were unconscious. The force of the explosion made them fly mid-way. Some impacted their heads to the ground very hard, and some bled.

Jedrek was the first to wake up as blood dripped from his forehead. He saw everyone, including Alesia, unconscious from the impact on the ground. They all escaped; a sigh escaped his lips. He slowly sat up and then heard a groan. Fred also woke up as he was bleeding everywhere.

Jedrek went to him. "Fred, how are you feeling?"

"Could be better." Fred slowly sat up with the help of Jedrek. Others began to wake up, but Alesia. Jedrek went to her and gently shook her, but she didn't wake up. He checked her pulse; she was still breathing. He let out a sigh of relief. He carried her, and the group helped one another get to their vehicles. However, many heard firefighters and other soldiers that survived and escaped the facility, and many were calling for backup.

Jedrek knew that the soldiers were looking for survivors. The higher-ups would get called and try to hide the situation and cause since they are part of the U.S. government. However, many witnesses saw him and the others. Many knew he was still free, and the government would not give up until he was found.

Everyone got to their vehicles. Jedrek gently put Alesia inside, but he didn't go inside. Fred noticed. "What are you doing? We have to go!"

Jedrek shook his head. "I can't go."

Many stilled as they got inside the vehicles. "What do you mean that you can't go? We need to leave now."

"Many know I am still alive and free and will inform their superiors. They also will know about Alesia and many of you. However, they will try to find and kill all of you. I can't let that happen."

Fred got out of the vehicle. "What are you trying to say?"

"I already told Leo. I made him promise to help care for Alesia and our unborn child. I also ask you to please watch and protect them. My mother and father died because of this corrupt government. I don't want Alesia and our child to go through fate. They will not stop until I am caught. I need to lead them away from my family and all of you. I will find a way to make us unforgotten or try to get them out of the way."

"What about Alesia!? She won't let you go that easy!?"

Jedrek smiled. "I know, but I'm doing this for her and our child. I'm doing this because I love her." He patted Fred on the shoulder. "Please, this is the one favor that I ask of you. Protect them. I hope that I will see them again one day, free."

All were silent until the noise of dogs and soldiers ordering to find survivors and culprits. They were getting close. "Go before they find you all." Fred could only nod as he got inside the vehicle and ordered everyone to head out. Jedrek watched as they all left. He bit his lower lip as he felt tears forming in his eyes. Jedrek didn't look back as he began to run and go into the shadows.

....

After the rescue, along with Leo, Fred, and the others went into hiding. When Alesia had awoken and asked for Jedrek, Fred and Leo informed her of what Jedrek wanted. She wanted to go to him, but Leo and Fred told her of their promise with Jedrek and that this was what he wanted.

This broke the young woman. It broke her heart, not knowing if they would see each other again.

They all knew that they were not clear. There were still survivors from the facility that would begin to look for them, but most importantly, for Jedrek. Months went by, and the group would move from place to place within the country. They knew it wouldn't be safe if Alesia gave birth in a hospital. It was challenging for Alesia, especially during her pregnancy. There were times when she would have severe sickness and pain. However, she felt fortunate for Leo and Fred, and the others. The plan was that a couple of months after Alesia gave birth, she, the baby, Leo, and the group were to move to another country.

Not to the group's surprise, the explosion was covered up in the news and kept the absolute truth of the facility hushed up. They knew that the government was involved in supporting the silence.

Months went and came. Alesia gave birth to a boy and named him Klaus. They all waited until the little boy was about eight months. Meanwhile, Fred and Leo decided that Alesia would go live in Switzerland. Leo knew many friends who were in the hacker group Anonymous. Many Anonymous members were excellent hackers who made a new identity for Alesia and the rest who would protect her.

Alesia was given a new identity and was granted citizenship in Switzerland along with her child. Luckily Leo wasn't seen in the facility, and it was easy for him to get through the radar. Fred, however, decided to stay in the U.S. to see if he could find anything on Jedrek and would keep Alesia updated.

Meanwhile, with the help of Leo and the others, they assisted her with her finances. Alesia would take classes to learn the language, raise her son, and take him to school and work. It was challenging for her, especially not knowing about Jedrek's whereabouts. There was no news of him.

Months then turned into years. Alesia raised her son with the help of Leo, Fred, and the other group members, who would visit from time to time. Her son, Klaus, who turned 25, grew up intelligent, hardworking, and respectful. He even had a girlfriend who he loved, and she loved him. However, he couldn't hide the truth from her about who he was. To Alesia and Klaus' surprise and relief, the young woman didn't fear him. Her love for Klaus was all that mattered.

While Klaus grew up, he inherited alien aspects from his father, especially his eyes. He was the spitting image of his father, but his skin tone was porcelain; his short light brown hair was wavy and nicely combed. Klaus was able to transform into an alien, but with some human aspects. Alesia eventually told Klaus about his father.

Everything.

Klaus was shocked at the least, but he understood. However, he was curious about his father and if he was alive. Fred didn't want to make Alesia lose hope, but since so many years had passed and there was no trace of Jedrek, he and the others felt that Jedrek may have been dead.

However, Klaus refused to believe so. He thought that his father may still be alive, and since he inherited his father's alien genes, he wanted to see if he could find him.

Klaus decided to go to the United States.

Alesia was afraid for his safety, but he assured his mother that he would be fine since he would have others to help Hed. He went with Fred, Leo and the others and Klaus pretended to go as a tourist.

It had almost been 30 days, and Alesia was worried; there was a part of her thought that Jedrek was gone. Maybe the government caught perhaps. Perhaps he died fighting or killed himself. Even though she looked strong for her son, she suffered sadness and worry for Jedrek. She never had the opportunity to say goodbye.

However, she knew that Jedrek would have been happy that she and their son lived a life of freedom and happiness, which he and his parents would have wanted. Jedrek broke the cycle of being a prisoner.

Klaus' girlfriend would stay with Alesia to await any news, but there wasn't any. However, two days ago, Klaus informed his girlfriend that he was returning home but not to tell his mother. She agreed.

At the moment, Alesia and Klaus' girlfriend decided to walk by a well-known park for its lakes. It was cold but doable. It was a nice change of pace for Alesia to keep her mind occupied with the negativity. However, Alesia could tell that something was off and asked about it. However, Klaus' girlfriend did not say but led her to the walking path. Alesia noticed a group standing on the track from afar as they both walked on.

The two women stopped, and Alesia's eyes widened as she saw her son, Fred, Leo, and their friends. Klaus smiled as his mother ran to him. He also ran to her. Mother and son hugged one another. "Klaus! I missed you! I was worried sick! My boy! My precious boy!"

They separated from the embrace as Klaus and his girlfriend hugged one another. Alesia, Fred, Leo, and the others hugged one another. Alesia then looked out to see if there was anyone else with them.

There was no one else.

Alesia felt pain in her heart. "He is gone..." she thought to herself. She couldn't contain the tears forming in her eyes. Everyone was silent. Klaus went to his mother and hugged her, and everyone gave them space.

From afar, there was a figure walking toward the group. His hair was short but well cut and groomed. He had a black heard and mustache. He had a broader build and had some cuts on his hands and parts of his face. He also had a slight limp, as if suffering an injury as he walked.

His footsteps were getting closer and closer. Klaus looked behind and let his mother go. She and the figure saw one another. Alesia felt her heart stop; tears overflowed. She cried. The figure stilled and extended his arms out with a smile. Tears were forming in his eyes. Alesia immediately ran towards him.

"JEDREK!" she cried.

"Alesia!"

Alesia jumped on him. Jedrek got a hold of her, and both were locked into each other's embrace. They cried as they hugged. Jedrek and Alesia were back together again. Jedrek thought he would never see her again as he hid from the enemy. His son found him. Now he is with the love of his life; his family. Klaus also went to hug his parents. Mother and father hugged their child.

Jedrek felt his tears becoming more rampant as he smiled. He had everything that he always wanted; his family.

He was finally free.